# LITTLE KATIA

**Based on**
**'The Story of a Little Girl'**
**by Catherine A. Almesdingen**
**1829–93**

For Helen.

" Happy Birthday "

Love from.

Auntie Eileen and

Uncle Stuart

*E. M. Almedingen*

# LITTLE KATIA

*London*
OXFORD UNIVERSITY PRESS
1971

*Oxford University Press, Ely House, London W.1*

GLASGOW  NEW YORK  TORONTO  MELBOURNE  WELLINGTON
CAPE TOWN  SALISBURY  IBADAN  NAIROBI  DAR ES SALAAM  LUSAKA  ADDIS ABABA
BOMBAY  CALCUTTA  MADRAS  KARACHI  LAHORE  DACCA
KUALA LUMPUR  SINGAPORE  HONG KONG  TOKYO

ISBN 0 19 272024 4

*To*

# IRENE WALDEGRAVE

*An affectionate token*
*for many years of friendship*

*Printed in Holland*
*Zuid-Nederlandsche Drukkerij N.V.*
*'s-Hertogenbosch*

# CONTENTS

# Author's Note

Catherine A. Almedingen was born in St. Petersburg in 1829. Her mother dying in 1834, the child was taken by a cousin, Sophie Berquovist, to a distant kinsman's estate near Kursk in Little Russia. Catherine spent six years there. On the death of her cousin she returned to her father who had since married again. He had already entered her at the Catherine Nobility College in Moscow, where she went in 1842 and left in 1846 as a gold medallist.

Some years later Catherine married Serge Syssoev, a landowner in the Tver Province, but the role of a châtelaine could not satisfy her. She never considered her education completed because of the gold medal and other honours received in Moscow. She carried on with her private studies —particularly history, languages and music. Her first literary efforts appeared in the sixties and they were mostly translations from English and French. Gradually, her house in Tver became a centre for all the literati. It was always the children who attracted her most. A woman of large means and wife of a wealthy man, Catherine Almedingen spent both time and money on 'giving a chance', as she called it, to children and young people of 'the unprivileged classes'.

In 1871 she prevailed upon her husband to leave the country for St. Petersburg for a time. Serge Syssoev's death, however, made Catherine decide to settle permanently in the capital. From then onwards, children's literature, such a Cinderella in Russia at the time, absorbed her utterly. She translated a number of English and American classics— *Little Lord Fauntleroy, East Lynne, Daisy Chain, Cometh up as a Flower, Misunderstood, Little Women, The Wide Wide World, Thrown Together,* and so on. She also wrote a number of her own books—in particular, *Life of Harriet Beecher Stowe, Aleut Islands, Napoleon and Russia*—and a short study of Abraham Lincoln, but it was *The Story of a Little Girl,* here given the title of *Little Katia,* which, coming out in 1874, firmly established Catherine Almedingen's reputation as a leading children's author. In 1881 she founded one of the finest children's monthlies in Russia, *Rodnik,* which continued to be published till the very end of 1917.

'She had no children of her own,' says her biographer. Madame Zharinzova, herself a noted children's author, 'but her whole heart was given to them. All who met her knew her to be their friend ... Her literary standards were very high ... "The first essential in a children's book must be its honesty ..." she once said at a contributors' meeting. "When you are honest, you realize that you cannot *write down* for children ..." To see her among them was a joy. She could talk to them and engage their interest—but she also knew how to listen to them. *The Story of a Little Girl* brought her hundreds of little correspondents, few of whom she ever met—but she answered all their letters and to all of them she became their *dorogáya Toetiá Kátia,* "dear Aunt Katia".'

In 1890 Catherine Almedingen became seriously ill. No cure was then known for her complaint. Her physical health worsened from month to month. Her mental energies remained unimpaired to the end. No longer able to hold either pen or pencil, Catherine dictated to her secretary—even on the morning of 16th December 1893, the day of her death.

She was my great-aunt. Though born in Russia, she was a foreigner by blood, her father being of an Austro-Bavarian parentage and his first wife, Catherine's mother, a Dane.

A. P. Chekhov, one of the contributors to *Rodnik,* and Leo Tolstoy considered *The Story of a Little Girl* to be one of the most honest, appealing and absorbing child-autobiographies. It was first published in 1874, rapidly became a best-seller, was translated into French and German, and remained an acknowledged classic and favourite among children of all social ranks in Russia until the 1917 Revolution.

The present version, the first to appear in English, is no verbal translation. For one thing, the original runs into nearly 350 pages of excessively small print, octavo. For another, Catherine Almedingen wrote her book for Russian readers. A great many details, mentioned very briefly, would be utterly unintelligible to foreign readers unless some amplification were given. But I have not changed the landscape painted by my great-aunt with great skill and deep affection. There are no invented scenes or characters in the original—but there is much dialogue, and in writing her story, Catherine Almedingen must have had recourse to the diaries kept by her since childhood. Nothing is exaggerated. To a child of her generation the theft of a few plums was a major crime indeed.

Catherine's memory was remarkable, but far more than memory was needed to write a book which was to win friends among more than one generation of children, and in adapting *The Story of a Little Girl* for English readers I have tried my utmost to recapture the climate of the original.

E. M. ALMEDINGEN

Brookleaze
Bath, Somerset
*June* 1965

## 1 *Alone in that big house . . .*

The forecourt of the house faced the river and the great wrought iron gates, which were nearly always closed, marked the end of the world for me. The house was so vast that on occasions I would lose my way in some passage or other, open a door, see an unfamiliar room, and stand rooted in terror lest a bear or a wolf were to spring at me from behind a curtain or a cupboard. The house was full of people, but I was alone—except for brief encounters with my nannie, Agatha, and very occasional visits of Monsieur Basil, my father's friend. There was a crowd of servants, but they were not even names or faces to me. The only one I can remember was a footman, Roman, because he would occasionally smuggle a cake or a little tart 'for the poor young lady'.

I was five at the time. There were four of us in the family, my father, my elder brother, Nicholas, myself, and baby Andrew, whose coming, as Agatha once told me, had cost my mother her life. I remember my mother's illness and funeral very mistily. Much more clearly can I see what had gone before: her beauty, her laughter, her pretty dresses, her dancing, and above all, her caresses and her violet-grey eyes looking into mine. She loved me so, I knew I was necessary to her, and I repaid her affection as ardently as I could.

Then all suddenly she was there no longer. I believe I thought that some thief or other had stolen her away, and there was nobody whom I could question. Had I gone to Agatha, she would have told me, as she did so often, that I was a silly little girl.

I was not neglected in the crude sense of the word. Either Agatha or a maid woke me, had me washed, dressed, fed, and put to bed. Every morning I was taken to the library. My father gave me a perfunctory kiss and said a few words, and I was glad to escape. Very often I would not see him again for the rest of the day. My elder brother, Nicholas, was very ill at the time. He had had an accident when out riding. From time to time surgeons came to operate on his right leg. Anaesthetics were unknown in 1834, and Nicholas's screams could be heard all over the house. A very foolish maid having told me that my brother was 'being cut up', I used to hide in some dark corner—so terrified was I lest one of those strange black-coated gentlemen might find me and decided that I, too, needed 'cutting up'.

Nicholas's room was out of bounds for me, but I used to steal in often enough when he happened to be asleep. His room was full of rare treasures. I did not covet the toys, but the books always drew me. I could not read. I longed to be taught, but there was nobody to teach me my letters. My library consisted of two shabby volumes long since discarded by Nicholas—*Stories from the Bible* and a pink-bound French book, *Huit Jours de Vacances*. I had no idea what either of those books was about, but I cherished them because of their engravings.

And then I had Mimi, an enormous wooden doll with an ugly face, its paint long since flaked off because of my frequent kisses. She was far too big to sleep in my cot, but I dragged her about everywhere, the library excepted. I even insisted on taking her into the carriage when Agatha had enough leisure to take me for a drive. I talked to Mimi by the hour. I decided that I must have a real home for her. In that enormous house I built one of my own. It was a corner of the ballroom, next to a big grandfather clock. I furnished it with an embroidered stool from the nursery and a red velvet cushion purloined from one of the drawing-rooms. I had no toys of my own but I arranged the two books between the footstool and the cushion. I placed Mimi on the cushion, had the stool for myself, and imagined that I was in the drawing-room, in a silk dress and brocade slippers, expecting guests to arrive.

'Sit up, Mimi,' I would say sternly, 'otherwise I will send you to bed. You are a big girl now—you should know how to behave.'

But one morning I just did not know what to do with myself. Agatha was swept off her feet—there was so much to do for Nicholas. It was raining hard and I could not get out into the garden. I had, I think, hoped to be taken for a drive, but I dared not ask Agatha. She was not cross that morning, but she just had no time for me. She pushed a few boiled sweets into my hand as I was making for my 'house' in the ballroom and said that I would have an apple-tart for dinner, but somehow that did not comfort me very much. Even

3

Mimi had little attraction for me that morning.

The house seemed very still. I had heard one footman say to another that my father was out. I also knew that Nicholas was very ill that day. The ballroom became an enemy country. I tiptoed out into the hall. It was empty. I climbed up the first flight and turned into a passage. A door to the left was open wide. I knew it was baby Andrew's nursery. I trotted in, a boiled sweet held tight in my little fist.

Andrew lay fast asleep in his blue-and-white beribboned cot. I came up and stared at him. It seemed strange to me that he should be sleeping so peacefully when, as Agatha had told me, it was his fault that someone had come and stolen my mother away.

And then Andrew woke up, looked at me, and stretched out one fat, tiny hand. 'He wants me,' I said to myself, and such a wave of gratitude and tenderness swept over me that I wished I might make some return to him. At once I remembered the big boiled sweet I still held in my hand.

'But his hand is so tiny he could never hold it,' I thought and, bending over, was just about to push the sweet into Andrew's mouth when his nurse came into the room. She saw what I was about. She screamed, ran and pulled me away from the cot. Agatha ran in, spanked me hard then and there, dragged me down the stairs, and brought me into the ballroom.

'You wicked little girl,' she went on scolding. 'Don't you know that you might have killed Andrew with that big sweet? If you ever dare go into his nursery again, I shall tell the master.'

'I did not mean to hurt Andrew,' I wept, 'and I got so bored, Nannie. There is nothing for me to do.'

'Nothing to do? Heavens above, child, you have that doll, you have your books.'

'Mimi was asleep,' I said sadly, 'and I can't read, Nannie.' I gulped hard. 'And everybody is always cross with me—'

'Because you keep doing silly things,' retorted Agatha.

4

'You know you are not to go near the kitchens. Who went there yesterday and upset a whole jugful of cream? And you will run off to the stables, too. Efim says you will tease the horses so. Goodness, child, I was up the whole night with Nicholas. I hear there is a hospital nurse coming to help, but she does not know Nicholas, and it will all fall on me in the end—and I am not as young as I was, child. And now stop crying! If the weather clears up, I might take you for a drive after dinner, and we'll go across the river.'

But the weather did not clear up and, anyway, Agatha was much too busy to think about a drive. It proved to be a black-letter day and there were many such.

Yet there were others, too. I liked Monsieur Basil's visits. Of course, he came to see my father, but he always spared me a few moments before leaving the house. He would bring me gifts—a small painted ball, an orange, or a little chocolate. He told me stories. It was from him that I learned the fairy-tales of Vassilissa the Beautiful and Ivan the Little Fool. Monsieur Basil was younger than my father and I believe he was a bachelor. I knew nothing much about him, but I liked him because he was so kindly. He played the guitar and he taught me to dance the *Rússkaya*.

Monsieur Basil came in the afternoon of what was the blackest day of all. Nicholas happened to be much worse. I hardly saw Agatha. A maid came to dress me. Someone remembered my breakfast, but my dinner was nearly forgotten, and in the end it came into the ballroom. A footman brought it on a little table, but all the gilt chairs in the room were much too high for me and I had to eat standing. When the man had cleared it all away, I imagined myself utterly lost and forgotten. I dared not leave my 'house' in the ballroom. I just sat there, crying my eyes out, and Monsieur Basil found me trying to dry my face on a very inadequate pinafore.

'What is the matter?' he asked at once.

'Nicholas is worse, and nobody wants me, and I don't

know what to do.'

'What about going for a drive?'

'Our coachman is ill.'

'Well, there is the garden—'

I hung my head. I was most reluctant to confess that I felt afraid of going into the garden all on my own—two great dogs, which really belonged to the stable-yard, used to run about there, and I was terrified of them.

'Why not go for a walk? It is so sunny and the streets are not dirty.'

'Nannie says young ladies should never go walking in the streets.'

'Well, then, what about dancing?'

'Yes, if you will play,' I said, my tears drying at once.

'Certainly.' And Monsieur Basil leapt off his chair and went to fetch the guitar which hung on a wall in the great hall.

He played the opening bars. I came out into the middle of the ballroom and curved my arm over my head as he had taught me. All my misery was gone. Someone liked me well enough to play the guitar for my pleasure. My tiny feet glided across the parquet, and I even smiled at Monsieur Basil as I passed him.

And then suddenly a door was opened wide. I saw my father stand there. I did not even know that he was at home. I stopped and my arm came down almost by itself. Tall, my father seemed even taller that day and his grey eyes looked cold and stern. I saw him throw a reproachful glance at his friend. Then he looked at me, and my world turned blacker than it had ever been before.

'Dancing?' He spoke icily. 'Your poor brother is worse. He is in great pain—and you dance!'

I cannot remember what happened after that except that I found myself all alone in the ballroom. I rushed to Mimi, hugged her wildly, and told her I wished that someone would come and steal me away for good. When, presently,

Agatha came in, I stamped my foot and ordered her to leave me. She took no notice.

'I knew there would be trouble with that guitar and all,' she said sombrely. 'The gentleman should have known better.'

I did not answer. I bent over Mimi and began re-tying her faded green sash.

'Now, child,' Agatha went on in an unfamiliarly soft voice, 'don't take on so! I know things are difficult, but everything will soon be changed for you once you have gone from here.'

I dropped Mimi, jumped to my feet and stared at Agatha.

'So someone is going to steal me?'

'Stop such nonsense, child! Who in the world would think of stealing you? It is your Cousin Sophie who is coming—all the way from St. Petersburg. She should have come here long before, but she was called away to some foreign parts—I don't rightly know where.'

'Who is she?'

'Why, your father's cousin, child.'

'Nannie, do you know her?'

'She came to the master's wedding'—Agatha spoke a little grimly—'and used to visit here sometimes—but never after you came, my dear. She is clever and strict, and she will have you taught your letters and everything. She is taking you away for good, child.'

I kept staring hard.

'But why—why?'

'Your mamma asked her to look after you,' explained Agatha. 'She is going to make you her heiress, see.'

I had no idea what the word meant and I asked no questions about it.

'Where does she live, Nannie?'

'Ah, several days' journey from here,' replied Agatha. 'And, I have heard folk say, in a far bigger house than ours— it belongs to another cousin, my dear.' Here she fumbled in one of her capacious pockets and pulled out a large piece of gingerbread. 'Here is something for you and don't you think hard of your old nurse. I do scold you and I spank you, too, but you are at home here. It will be a bit different *there*. Your Cousin Sophie is strict. You will have to behave, child, and not rush into any tantrums. Ah yes, you will remember your old Agatha and wish you had her with you.'

'Does Papa know I am going?' I asked suddenly, and Agatha laughed.

'Goodness, it was the master himself who made all the arrangements, my dear.'

'What do you mean, Nannie?'

'Why, your Cousin Sophie is going to adopt you. Didn't I say she will make you her heiress? And there are many papers to write and to sign about such things.'

I understood none of that, but the skies were certainly widened for me that day. I was excited and more than a little frightened, too. Where was I going? Who were the other cousins? I knew none of my relations. Would there be any other children? Would I be allowed to keep Mimi? Was baby Andrew coming with us? What was Cousin Sophie really like? I spent the whole of that afternoon talking to Mimi. In the end I turned away from her and asked God if He could not turn my doll into a real little girl. There was so much to find out. Agatha's chatter had left a cloud in my mind, and I longed for clarity. So I began building one picture after another in my imagination. Sometimes Cousin Sophie was a princess in a black velvet gown with foamy cream lace on her head, sometimes she was a witch in the Vassilissa story, and she ended by resembling the ill-tempered cadaverous nurse, with a mole on each cheek, who came and helped Agatha to look after Nicholas.

Presently, my imagination got tired, and I stepped back into the very small world I knew. I thought of my father, of Nicholas on his sick-bed, of little Andrew, even of Agatha and of Roman, the footman, and Efim, the head coachman.

Would I go far away and never see any of them again? I could not tell.

I remember how, the very day after, I hid in the corner of the great hall and waited for my father to come out of the library. When he appeared, my heart all but missed a beat. He turned his back and began winding his watch in front of the hall clock. Then, the watch wound, he stood there, his hands at his back. He had not seen me at all. I crept out of my little lair, tiptoed across, and dropped a kiss on the palm of his left hand. He swung round at once.

'Ah, Katia—' his voice rang gentle. 'Your brother is so much better today. Is there something you wanted?'

Dear me, I wanted such a lot! I wanted him to pick me up in his arms, to kiss me, to say that he loved me. I wanted to tell him that I loved him terribly for all my awe of him. But I stood rooted, my cheeks scarlet, and I never said a word. He smiled a little distantly, patted my head, and went out.

I was then too small to be told that my mother's death had left him frozen. Had I heard any such thing, I would not have understood it.

I cannot now remember how long it was before Cousin Sophie arrived, but from that day my life became an unending misery to myself and to the entire household. I no longer kept to the ballroom. I wandered about, getting into everybody's way, and hardly a day passed but Agatha had to spank me for some mischief or other. Every morning I got up, expecting something to happen. I imagined myself now a foundling, now a fairy-tale princess, now a victim of everybody's dislike. Little wonder that the household despaired of me. I pulled up flowers in the garden, upset things in the kitchens, tore my pinafores to shreds, made fearful noises outside Nicholas's door, and little Andrew's nurse declared that she could not leave him for an instant for fear of my running in and doing him some mischief. Once I managed to open a window and to pour a jugful of cold water on the head of a laundry-maid, a perfectly harmless country-girl.

9

And all the time I nursed the idea that I was being perse-cuted from morning till night.

The household grumbled. Agatha kept punishing me, but nobody ever complained to my father.

And, at last, Cousin Sophie arrived, and she was not a bit what I imagined she would be!

## 2 *Such a strange, wonderful world . . .*

It happened one evening in early spring, and the great chandelier in the hall was lit in honour of the guest. I should have been in bed long ago, but I stood on the lowest step of the stairs, and nobody took any notice of me, not even Agatha, whose small brown eyes were riveted on the front door. I saw my father move forward, the door was flung open, and a plump, fresh-faced woman stood there. Her violet bonnet and dark grey cloak were certainly a disappointment, since I had expected a princess in velvet and jewels, but when Cousin Sophie crossed the hall and stooped to kiss me, I saw her very clear blue eyes, and I said to myself, 'I could never tell *her* a fib.' Her kiss had both warmth and restraint, and I certainly liked her quiet voice:

'Well, Katia, I am glad you stayed up to meet me, and now we must say good night.'

In an instant I found myself climbing the stairs to my bedroom, my hand clutching Agata's roughened fingers, and Agatha was oddly silent. I suppose she felt utterly out of her depth: never before had I gone to bed without endless arguments and tears.

Such, then, was the beginning, and within a few days the house became a new and exciting country. Cousin Sophie gave no orders but somehow all the servants, even the stubborn Agatha, did whatever she wanted them to do. I no longer had my meals in the day-nursery but ate in the dining-room, and my 'house' in the ballroom was untenanted. A small chair was put specially for me in one of the drawing-rooms, and there I spent hours with my future foster-mother, whose finely shaped hands were never idle. There was the matter of my wardrobe; most of my frocks greatly displeased her, and she charged herself to make me a new outfit. My red shoes which I wore on Sundays were at once judged unsuitable and, to my sharp grief, were given to a laundress's daughter. My hair was carefully brushed out by Cousin Sophie, and Agatha was no longer allowed to curl it. I was rather glad to see the end of the curling-tongs.

There were no more visits of Monsieur Basil, but I did not miss him. I was in the very heart of a tremendous change and every day brought new discoveries. There was not a moment left for tantrums. I no longer wandered from room to room or sat in some corner, telling Mimi that I was the most wretched and the most unwanted little girl in the world. Cousin Sophie was still a stranger but something told me that I already meant much to her. One day after dinner she told me that my mother had asked her to look after me.

'But, you see, I was in Denmark at the time. An old uncle needed me.'

'Are we going far away?' I asked shyly.

'Oh yes, to Little Russia, but I don't suppose you know where that is. You will have three little cousins to play with and you will all have lessons together.'

This was something utterly new. I had never had a play-mate in my life. But I did not say so.

'By the way,' Cousin Sophie went on, plying her needle so swiftly that the dark yellow thread moved like lightning, 'you know your letters, of course?'

I blushed scarlet and shook my head.

'Oh, Katia, this is dreadful! Why, little Kolia at Trost-nikovo is the same age as you, and he can read and write, too. Nina, who is two years older, can read and write in two languages, and so can Volodia. Well, we must certainly put it right, my child.'

And at that moment my father came into the room. Cousin Sophie stopped hemming my petticoat, looked up and said something rather sharply in French. He answered in the same language, and her voice was coloured with quiet but unmistakable anger. He sighed, shrugged, and went out of the room. I knew that he had been scolded and I felt rather unhappy.

'I will learn my letters, Cousin Sophie,' I stammered.

'Please call me "Mamma",' she said. 'I have already said that you are going to be my little daughter.'

I had heard about it from Agatha, but the word would not come to my lips for a long time.

Cousin Sophie neither hustled nor bustled, but she got everything ready very rapidly. A yellow trunk was bought for my new wardrobe, and a new pink bonnet somewhat reconciled me to the loss of the red shoes. Every morning Agatha appeared upset, and grumbled while doing my hair which she no longer was allowed to curl.

'It is a foreign country you will be going to, child, and there will be nobody to pet you. It will be lessons and lessons without end, and no pudding for supper, either. I must say some people are hard-hearted. Yes, the day will come when you will miss your old Agatha.'

I did not think so. In a sense I had already gone from the house. I had not the least sense of regret at leaving my father, my two brothers, Agatha and the other servants. I was not quite sure if I loved Cousin Sophie but I felt that I could trust her. She was like a key to open many doors.

Many things were certainly difficult to learn. I was told not to swing my legs when sitting on a chair, not to slouch, or ruffle my hair, or lick the window-panes, a pastime to which my long spells of boredom had rather accustomed me. The first time Cousin Sophie saw me stamp my foot at a servant, she at once took me into her room and told me to apologize to the man.

'It is rude to stamp your foot at anyone. To do that to a servant is worse than rude—it is mean, because the man can't answer back.'

It was such a novel idea that I stared and mumbled:
'But—but Roman is a footman.'
'Precisely because he is a footman,' said Cousin Sophie.
All suddenly it was my last evening at home. I had my supper earlier than usual and Cousin Sophie took me to the library to say good night to my father. He looked up and opened his arms.
'Let her sit on my knees for a moment,' he said, and those few words were enough to open my heart, which had hungered and thirsted for his affection so long. I scrambled up to his knees, flung both arms round his neck, showered wild kisses all over his face, and then burst into tears.
'Now you have upset her, Alexis,' said Cousin Sophie. 'She will have a bad night and be anything but fit for the journey—'
'No, no, cousin,' replied my father, answering my kisses with his own. Then he rose and carried me up the stairs. I went on sobbing. Cousin Sophie did not ring for Agatha but undressed and washed me herself, put me to bed, covered me up, and said very sternly:
'Now, that is enough, child. Stop crying and go to sleep.'
Within a few minutes I was fast asleep.
The Moscow coach was to come in the morning, and they called me very early. Agatha, her eyes swollen, dressed me. I felt as though I were moving about in a mist. Nothing seemed real. Even my new brown cashmere dress felt strange to the touch. After breakfast, it was time to say good-bye. I did so quite mechanically, moving from room to room like a marionette. I did not even take a last glimpse at the ballroom: I was so impatient to get away. Only when I came into Nicholas's room did my eyes fill with tears, and he, who had always been so remote and indifferent, burst into sobs. I ran into the nursery and covered Andrew's tiny face with such vehement kisses that his nurse had to take me away from the cot. But when I got downstairs, all feeling

had gone. I said good-bye to my father in the collected manner of a prim, well-brought-up little girl going off for a short holiday. He put me into the coach and shook hands with Cousin Sophie.

'Take care of her, cousin,' he said, his voice a little unsteady, and she smiled at him.

'Don't worry, Alexis. I shall write often and take every care of her and bring her back to you some day.'

The postilion sounded the horn once again and the enormous coach moved out of the courtyard. Some impulse made me lean out of the window and wave my hand towards the porch.

Never before had I travelled in a coach. Drawn by eight horses and divided into four separate berths, it seemed a moving house to me. I admired all its numberless flap pockets, the little folding table for meals, and the funny contrivance of straps and buckles on its roof, Cousin Sophie explaining that it held a mattress and bedding.

'Don't we stop at a house to sleep?'

'Not till we get to Moscow,' she smiled.

It was all novel and certainly exciting, but the novelty thinned out soon enough. We were travelling in spring and the roads were shocking, with deep ruts here and there made by the usual spring floods. I got tired and bored long before we came to the first post-station along the route, and a particularly violent bump made me knock my knee against a dressing-case. The knee was not really hurt but I decided that it was and wailed loudly.

'What is the matter?' Cousin Sophie put down her book.

'I have hurt my knee,' I mumbled, and went on howling.

She at once undid my garter and examined the supposedly afflicted limb.

'It can't really hurt, Katia, can it?'

I sniffed.

'And I want to go home.'

'My dear, we are a long way from Tver now. To return

15

would be impossible. Moreover, your home is with me. I have explained it all.'

'I don't want to come to you,' I yelled. 'I hate you. I want Papa and Nicholas and Andrew and Agatha. I hate you,' and I jumped from my seat down on the hamper at Cousin Sophie's feet. But the hamper proved unpleasantly hard and I scrambled up to the seat again and started kicking at the little folding-table. Cousin Sophie watched me in silence. When I looked up, I saw her smile, and wildness swept over me. If I had known how to open the coach door, I suppose I would have jumped out on to the road. As it was, I seized poor Mimi, knocked her head against a piece of luggage, pulled her hair, and went on screaming.

'Leave the poor doll alone,' Cousin Sophie said at last. 'She has done nothing to annoy you, and she at least is not crying. Your face is all black.'

I scowled and dropped Mimi on the floor. Cousin Sophie sat in silence. At last, I raised my face. Her smile drew me towards her. She settled me in her lap and said very gently:

'Don't make me ashamed of you, dearest. Why, our neighbours in the next berth must have thought that you were being beaten. Nobody should scream like that.'

Ashamed, I closed my eyes. She tickled the tip of my nose with her gloved finger. I mumbled that I was sorry and fell asleep in her arms.

We stayed in Moscow for nearly three weeks and by the time we left, Cousin Sophie ceased being a stranger. The word 'Mamma' was still hard to say and I avoided using it, but I grew very attached to her and she won my heart wholly the day she began teaching me my alphabet. Within a few hours I learned to distinguish consonants from vowels and by the time we left Moscow, I could make up short words without any help. Cousin Sophie's delight knew no bounds when she discovered that her adopted daughter was not stupid.

The journey south from Moscow was really terrible.

16

There were many rivers to cross by ferry and I was so terrified of the water that I sat with eyes shut tight and my fingers
to my ears. As we came nearer and nearer to Kursk, the
roads were well-nigh impassable for the mud left by the
floods.

I cannot remember our arrival at Trostnikovo. I could not
open my eyes for sheer weariness. Someone got me out of
the coach and carried me up the stairs. I must have been put
to bed. I knew nothing until Cousin Sophie's clear voice
called just above my head:

'Katia, it is time you were up!'

I opened my eyes, imagining that we were still on the
road. I saw a large sunlit room, its walls a warm brown, its
pale green curtains embroidered with hunting-scenes. I saw
a flower-study framed in gold, a comfortable sofa, some
armchairs, and my yellow trunk open on the floor, and I
realized that the long journey was over and that I had come
—home.

Yes! I had spent no more than six weeks with Cousin
Sophie, but I no longer thought about Tver, our house there
and my family. All of it was over. Now I was truly at home
—in a strange house—with my cousins Mirkov whom I had
not yet met. It sounds nonsense but it was not.

A door opened. I saw a little girl, slightly older than myself, and behind her a beautiful woman in a white dressing-
gown, her loosely plaited auburn hair reaching below her
knees. They seemed strangers and yet they were not strangers. All the same, I slipped down on the pillows and pulled
up the blanket.

'Sophie,' said the woman in white, 'how very thin she is.
Is she delicate?'

'Not at all. She is perfectly fit. You remember her mother,
don't you? Christine was never plump. Now, Katia, here is
Nina, your little cousin.'

Nina had big grey eyes, two dimples and a most engaging
smile. Unprompted, she ran up to my bed and kissed me so

17

warmly that I felt I indeed belonged there.

Cousin Sophie smiled.

'And that is your Cousin Marie, Katia. Make her love you—she and I are great friends.'

I looked at my newly found cousin. Never had I seen anyone so beautiful, and I cannot describe her. The auburn hair, the great grey-blue eyes, the lovely mouth, the smile, the grace of her movements—all about Nina's mother filled me with such rapture that I just sat and stared. I had no idea there could be such people in the world.

'Don't you want to give me a kiss?' she asked. 'Why, I feel almost jealous.'

I at once leapt out of bed into her arms. The sun caught at the rich glints in Cousin Marie's hair and I felt as though I had come into an enchanted kingdom. I was so small that I could not give a detailed account of my feelings at the time, but I know that I felt warm and safe and happy.

It was Nina who took me to breakfast that first morning at Trostnikovo. We went through several landings and corridors before we came to the stairs. Below, at the end of a short passage, two boys stood waiting for us. They were dressed in blue cotton blouses and white pantaloons. The taller of the two was fair and seemed rather delicate. The younger—about the same age as myself—was dark, with very sharp black eyes and something of a challenge in his face. Both boys clicked their heels when they saw us.

'Oh, you sillies,' laughed Nina. 'She is not a visitor. She is our cousin Katia. Now then, kiss her,' she commanded. But the younger boy whistled and ran off. The other, whose name was Volodia, bowed and offered me his arm.

'Let us go and have breakfast,' he said very politely, and Nina laughed again.

'Oh, Volodia, really . . . must you play at being a grown-up? Come on, Katia, we'd better run.'

We ran, but Trostnikovo was so vast that I wondered how long it would take to reach the dining-room. At last we got there, and it took me a few moments to get my bearings. There was a very long table presided over by a housekeeper in a tall white cap. There were some gentlemen and elderly ladies busily eating their breakfast. There was a plump nurse in a beribboned white coif, a rosy-cheeked baby in her lap. There was Kolia, all excited gestures, talking to a tall, slim man in a pale grey coat, with a pipe in his mouth. There was so much light, talk, movement and laughter that I felt lost and wished Cousin Sophie were there. Kolia looked towards the door and shouted:

'And here she is, Papa—'

The tall man was my cousin, Nicholas Mirkov. He turned, smiling broadly, and Nina ran forward.

'Papa, Papa, Mamma and I were in Cousin Sophie's room, and Katia thought Mamma's hair was lovely, and—'

'Now then, stop, you little chatterbox,' said my Cousin Nicholas, and he stooped, picked me up, kissed me on both cheeks, and turned to the woman at the head of the table. 'Amalie, for goodness' sake give her a good breakfast. She is as light as a feather—nothing but skin and bone.'

A mug of milk and some food were put before me. Nina, her mother not being there, played hostess, but I could hardly eat and drink. My head was almost going round. Kolia, his own breakfast unfinished, started running round the table, whistling and shouting at the top of his voice. Nina and Volodia were chattering away with their father. He kept puffing at his pipe, tickling each of them in turn, and laughing at their nonsense. I felt lost, excited and happy all at once. It was so unlike anything I had ever known.

Here Cousin Sophie came in and Nina leapt to her feet.

'Cousin Sophie, may we show Katia the park and the waterfall?' she cried. 'It is a holiday, isn't it?'

Cousin Sophie sat down at the table.

'Well, not quite a holiday, my dear—at least not for the boys.'

'But there is plenty of time till our first lesson,' Volodia

19

and Kolia cried chorally. Permission was given and Nina, clutching me by the hand, led the way out to the long terrace. The garden spread to the right and the left of the house, but the terrace steps led to a wide avenue of thick-girthed birches. As soon as we were in the avenue, I heard such an unfamiliar noise overhead that I asked if it was the waterfall.

'No, Katia. The waterfall is at the end of the park. You would not hear it from here.'

'But what is the noise?' I asked.

They laughed.

'Why, it is the wind in the park,' said Kolia. 'Papa says the park is like a forest.'

'Here, to the left, is the maze—' Volodia turned to me— 'but don't go there, Katia—so many frogs—'

'Don't listen to him,' Kolia broke in. 'There is a lovely spot in the maze, Katia. I'll take you there.'

'And the frogs?' I asked timidly.

'You are afraid of frogs?' He laughed. 'Oh, goodness— just like Volodia!'

'Please don't be such a tease, Kolia,' begged Nina, and she started telling me about a fire they had had the year before. 'And all the hothouses were burned down. There, to the right, are the orchards and beyond them the lake and the kitchen-gardens. Now, see that clump of weeping-willows to the left? We may not go there.'

'Why?' And I knew that I wanted to go there and nowhere else.

'There is a very deep well and its railings haven't been mended.'

'Nikita the groom got drowned there,' added Volodia, and Kolia turned to me.

'Let's run and see it, Katia, shall we?'

'You mustn't, Kolia.' Nina looked horrified. 'Papa said we were not to.'

'Well, you do what you like—but I am going.'

20

Volodia tried to stop him by catching hold of his belt, but Kolia would not give in, and the two boys started a fight. Nina was horrified, but I watched, all my sympathies on Kolia's side. The battle finished with poor Volodia getting his ears boxed so violently that he tumbled down.

'Kolia, Kolia,' Nina shouted. 'What a shame! What will Katia think of you? Hitting your brother like that!'

'He started it, didn't he?' Kolia retorted.

'And you fight like a stable-boy,' Volodia whimpered, wiping his face.

'Go on, go on, you cry-baby! High time they dressed you in a girl's clothes,' mocked Kolia and ran on ahead, and I knew I liked him immensely.

The avenue went on and on. Presently we found ourselves in the park. Its immensity, the soughing of wind in the tree branches, and the roar of the waterfall—heard from quite a distance—all those together frightened me. I tried not to show it, but I clutched Nina's hand harder and harder. We ran up a little hillock—with something of a narrow ride seen to the right. Beyond it stretched an immense tapestry of coral-red, white and pink of the orchards. Still farther away a mass of lilacs in full bloom so attracted me that I wished we could have stopped then and there. That morning I had my very first glimpse of the country, and I saw it at its best —in May—with the sun turning both park, orchard and gardens into an incredible glory.

But my little cousins hurried on towards the waterfall, the first I was to see. We went down a few stone steps and sat on a bench. That foaming, flounced mass of water falling into a miniature lake was certainly a marvel, but it made me tremble, and I asked to be taken back.

My cousins were delighted with the impression the park and the waterfall had made on me.

It was a very long walk back to the house, and my little legs were rather weary. My cousins did not know that I had never seen the country before and that my walks had been taken in a garden—big enough for a town house but tiny by comparison with the immensity I now saw all round me.

When we got back, Volodia went to have a lesson with his tutor, and Nina and I went to Cousin Sophie's room, where she helped me unpack the few treasures I had been allowed to bring with me. The house and the grounds—indeed, everything—seemed far too immense, but Nina, the very first playmate I had ever had, proved a dear friend from the first day.

## 3 *My first roots*

I find that I cannot tell season from season of my first year at Trostnikovo. The impressions it left were certainly deep, and there must have been many things happening—I still remember a few of them—but all in all that first year seems rather like a plunge into a lake so tranquil that one could float about and take in the banks embroidered with lovely flowers, the song of an unseen lark, the poise of a heron, and the calm of a cloudless sky.

I was a very distant cousin of the Mirkovs, but from the very first day the children looked upon me as their sister. Soon enough the slightly formal 'Cousin Nicholas' and 'Cousin Marie' were changed for the warm 'Uncle' and 'Aunt'. I shared Nina's bedroom, and Fat Dasha, a maid, whose corpulence was laughed at in many neighbouring villages, looked after us both. Cousin Sophie and Aunt Marie seemed all in all to each other, and soon enough I began to marvel at my adopted mother's genius in running such an immense household. Aunt Marie, alas, would not have known how to manage a rabbit-hutch. Summer and winter, Cousin Sophie was up at six, had a cold tub, went all over the house, received the head servants and gave the day's orders, visited kitchens, store-rooms and larders. About eight she called Nina and me, almost always watched Fat Dasha maiding us, heard our prayers, and took us in to breakfast. We had lessons with her till noon, when a light meal was served in a small room behind the hall.

Luncheon over, we were sent into the garden—whatever the weather. We were free to play games, to run about, or to help in the vast kitchen-gardens, but we were to stay out of doors till three which was our dinner-hour. When it rained, we had all our clothes changed on coming in, and I cannot remember any of us ever sneezing, sniffing, still less coughing. The coming of winter made no difference to this part of the day's routine except that we were sent out dressed very warmly. It all sounds rather Spartan, and it was meant to be.

The dinner over, Cousin Sophie devoted some time to me alone. Then she wrote letters and worked at her translations of articles on education and literary matters from Swedish, Danish and Italian. She used to send those articles to St. Petersburg, where they got published in some of the most important reviews of the day. With it all, Cousin Sophie found time to read aloud to us children and to join Aunt Marie in the drawing-room whenever there were visitors—and that, I think, happened almost every day. Cousin Sophie's life was one of endless activity. Never did I see her idle. Even when walking in the garden, she would either do tatting or knit stockings as fine as lace. Our own day finished at eight precisely. We knew that the grown-ups sat down to supper either at nine or ten. It must have been late when Cousin Sophie retired to her own room, but her energies never flagged.

It was odd that she and Aunt Marie should have been so close to each other. They seemed to have nothing in common—on the surface. Aunt Marie was every inch a society woman of her day. Her coiffure and her gowns were a pleasure to look at. She liked reading but confined it to French novels, Balzac being her favourite. She had a fine voice and often sang in the evenings. She was fond of flowers but her care for them found no other expression than a fleeting daily visit to the hothouses filled with exotic and expensive plants ordered from Riga and Hamburg. Any serious occupation, be it some utilitarian needlework or care for the household, was to her unthinkable. To an outsider,

24

Aunt Marie would have appeared no more and no less than an exquisite figurehead, but the entire household worshipped her—not only because of her singular beauty but because of her equally incredible gentleness. She stood as mediator between her husband and his serfs. Never once did I hear her voice raised in reproach, never did I see a frown on that lovely face. Intensely happy with her husband and children, Aunt Marie seemed to have made a vow never to cause the least misery to her neighbour.

Sometimes she came into the classroom to give us what she thought was a French lesson. It was pure pleasure to her and to us, too. She joked and laughed, and turned the dullest dictation into an entertainment. Her arm round someone's shoulders, she would begin '*J'ai vu hier une petite chatte . . .*' then turn to me. 'Did you hear that, Katia? "*Une petite chatte.*" Perhaps the words refer to you—you are just like a kitten—ready to scratch if you don't get your own way—', and I would burn scarlet since it was, alas, only too true, but Aunt Marie would laugh and we would all know she had been joking.

An impenetrable wall divided our own little world from that of the grown-ups. Crowds of visitors came to Trostnikovo, some for a meal, others for a prolonged stay, but we did not meet all of them. We had our lessons, our games, and our own guests. We never fed in the big dining-room except on so-called ordinary days with none but the family and a few intimates at the table. We were seldom allowed to join the grown-ups in any of the drawing-rooms. Parts of the big flower-garden were out of bounds for us.

It may all seem rather heavily regimented. It was not really. We were so busy that there was no time to get bored. And what fun we had, particularly when Uncle Nicholas was free to join in our games. He was especially clever at contriving 'surprises', fireworks on a lawn, a mushroom hunt in the nearest forest, a fishing expedition to Dnieprovka, a hamlet about ten miles away, where fine carp had their home in a lake. Yet those occasions did not come very often. Had Uncle Nicholas had his own way, he would have arranged a treat for every day, but Cousin Sophie would never have heard of it.

He adored his wife, loved his children, and grew very fond of me, but his strictness, not to say harshness, with the servants and peasants on the estate came to shock me as I grew older. He never raised his voice, but on more than one occasion I would see a cook or a footman go white at the few words spoken by Uncle Nicholas in a voice so low that I could not catch the words.

And one evening Nina and I were the unwitting witnesses of a painful scene in the library. We opened the door very softly. Aunt Marie was standing by the window, tears in her eyes and in her voice. We remained rooted and we heard her say:

'Nicholas, I beg you to forgive the man. He is so young —almost a boy. He did not mean to be rude.'

Nina and I should have coughed or made a movement. We just could not. And I barely recognized Uncle Nicholas— so sombre and stony did his face look, so cold was his voice:

'Please stop, Marie. The matter is settled. I said I'd do it and I shall do it. Andrew has asked for it. I hear the next recruitment is in the early autumn, and he is going.'

Here Uncle Nicholas became aware of us and the stoniness at once vanished in a smile:

'Ah, children, come to say good night? Yes, it is time. I heard the clock strike eight a few minutes ago.'

Aunt Marie kept wiping her eyes. We felt puzzled and very ill at ease, but we asked no questions, nor do I remember Nina and I discussing it between ourselves, though, of course, we had an idea that there had been some trouble on the estate. The very meaning of the word 'recruitment' was unknown to us. In those days, there was no conscription in Russia; the ranks of the army were filled by more or less irregular recruitments made compulsory in time of war.

26

Over and above that, any landowner had power to send serfs into the army as a punishment. The service lasted twenty-five years, if not longer. The discipline was cruel and the hardships so many that not all the recruits ever came home again. But, of course, we knew nothing of such things at the time.

A few months of a busy and ordered life made a different girl of me. I was never alone, I had much affection showered on me, and I had no leisure to imagine myself miserable. Within my first four months at Trostnikovo I learnt to read and write in Russian and French, and began arithmetic, history and geography. Glad to have found such a promising pupil in her adopted daughter, Cousin Sophie began increasing both the scope and the number of my daily lessons. I believe that she was getting proud of me. Yet there were traits in my character which made her nearly despair—in particular my obstinacy and a passion for wriggling out of the consequences of some minor misdeed or other.

One day, the morning lessons over, we four decided that it would be fun to build a little wooden boat and to send it down the stream. Kolia and Mirza—a little Tartar boy who was a page in the house—ran off to the carpenter's shop for wood, hammer and nails. Nina, Volodia and I waited for them on the steps of the terrace, when Cousin Sophie called me into the house.

'I have no time to do geography with you this afternoon, Katia. Come and let us do it now.'

'Have a heart, Sophie,' protested Uncle Nicholas. 'It is barely an hour since they finished their morning lessons. Look how thin Katia is! Aren't you working her too hard? I'd be in despair if Nina got like that.'

'Katia thin? Well, no wonder, she is growing rather fast,' answered Cousin Sophie. 'Come, child! The quicker we start the better.'

'Beastly, beastly geography,' I thought, following her to the schoolroom.

I had started on Europe about a week before. I knew the capitals, the main rivers and mountains of most countries. I even knew the names of all the reigning sovereigns. But that day I just could not think of Europe at all. The capitals were all right, but I began slipping over the rivers, and when we came to the mountains, I heard my dear Kolia's eager voice shouting, 'Nina, Katia, everything is ready. Come on . . .', and at once my mind flew to the stream and the little boat I would not see that day, and I promptly told Cousin Sophie that the Pyrenees were in Italy.

'Katia,' she exclaimed impatiently, 'how can you? You knew all the mountains yesterday. Now show me the Apennines—'

Most reluctantly I drew a line down Italy.

'That is better. Now, who is the King of France?'

'Louis-Philippe,' I muttered even more reluctantly, and heard Nina's laughter from a distance.

'And of Spain?'

'I don't know,' I replied after a pause.

Cousin Sophie's face went patchily red. I knew she was angry. I did not care.

'Of course you do. Why, only yesterday you had all the names at your finger-tips.'

'I don't know,' I repeated.

She looked at me and I looked at her. Through the widely opened window the scent of roses came into the room. I turned my head and stared at the big map on the wall.

'Katia, I am asking you for the last time—who is the King of Spain?' Now Cousin Sophie's voice was icy.

I pursed my lips by way of an answer.

'All right, then.' She got up. 'You will have no dinner today and you will stay here till I come for you.'

I just sat there like a wooden doll. She shook her head, sighed and left the room, and I heard the key turn in the lock. I scrambled on to the window-sill and began staring at the rose-garden, but my thoughts were not with the flowers.

'She does not love me at all . . . She would never punish

me like that—' the thought went wheeling round and round in my mind until the window-sill got too uncomfortable for my knees. I jumped down and went to sit on a sofa. Time passed. Nobody came to the door. It seemed as though I were all alone in that huge house—so quiet was it in the classroom. Presently, through the opened window I heard teasing sounds of silver and glass from the dining-room. I remembered Uncle Nicholas saying that we were to have a new strawberry pudding for dinner that day. Tears sprang to my eyes. When my handkerchief got soaked, I began rubbing my face with the pinafore. We happened to be in mourning for some distant cousin, and my pinafore was black. There hung a small mirror over the sofa. I stood on tiptoes and contemplated a streakily black, swollen face and tousled hair. My tears ran faster and faster. Hunger bit into me. I hated the King of Spain, Cousin Sophie and myself.

Then suddenly the door opened. Cousin Sophie and Aunt Marie came into the room. I did not get up. I just huddled on the sofa, my hair all over my face.

'Little kitten, ask Mamma to forgive you. She herself did not eat any dinner because of you.'

'Katia does not care one little bit.'

'Oh no, no, Sophie. Just look at her—all bedraggled and in tears. I am sure she is deeply sorry. You naughty, naughty little kitten,' said Aunt Marie, and she raised my head and kissed my dirty forehead.

Truth to tell, I did not feel in the least sorry and had no wish to ask pardon, but I was so hungry and it pleased me that my miserable appearance should have created such an impression on Aunt Marie.

Meanwhile Cousin Sophie crossed the room, sat down by me, laid her hand on my shoulder, and asked:

'And who is the King of Spain?'

'Ferdinand VII,' I replied in a barely audible whisper, and at that moment Uncle Nicholas came in.

'Gracious,' he cried, 'are you still fussing about that tiresome King of Spain? Why, poor Katia is all black and yellow with misery. Let her have some food at once and then send her out into the garden.'

I was washed, fed and sent off to play. Nina threw her arms round my neck and said she was so sorry. Volodia looked slightly uncomfortable, but my dear Kolia winked and whispered in my ear, 'I am sure you knew the name all the time. Well done!' But not one of my little cousins had the unkindness to tell me about the fun they must have had with the little boat down by the stream, and I felt grateful.

It was a few days later that a piece of really tremendous news came into the schoolroom. Aunt Marie broke it to us. We were to have a governess.

'She is a German lady from Dorpat. All of us are dining out today and you children must receive Mademoiselle Berg and do the honours of the house.'

We were exceedingly pleased at the idea of being hosts to a grown-up person—but the prospect of having a governess was far from pleasant.

It was raining hard that afternoon. We four found refuge in the Blue Room, which had no other furniture except three huge sofas and a mammoth mahogany bookcase full of books we were forbidden to read. The bookcase was never locked, and it certainly flattered us that the grown-ups trusted our honour to such an extent. I cannot remember a single occasion of any among us breaking the ban.

Why was the governess coming at all? Was she old or young? Would she be terribly strict?

'Now,' said Nina, 'I remember Mamma saying to Papa one day that Cousin Sophie had really a bit too much on her hands.'

'Kolia and I have our tutor,' Volodia pointed out.

'But Katia and I could not be taught by him,' Nina told him, and Kolia said sombrely:

'Of course not, and anyhow he is leaving before the winter.

I heard him say so to Papa. But whatever that woman is, I shan't love her.'

'Well, I am going to,' said Volodia. 'She is our neighbour and we are told to love all our neighbours.'

Now I was very fond of Volodia but I had no use for that sort of talk. He was apt to be far too prim for his age, and we all laughed at him.

'Good heavens,' Kolia shouted, 'what will you say next? Love the whole world, I suppose—I never could.'

'But—' his brother began, when we heard the bells of a *tróyka* and ran helter-skelter into the hall. Ivan, the butler, a solemn, white-haired man, always in tails and a snowy jabot, barred our way to the porch.

'A governess should not be spoiled, sir,' he said to Volodia.

We dared not argue with old Ivan. We waited breathlessly. Presently a very tall, fair, middle-aged woman came through the door. She looked plain and her face was covered with freckles. She was wrapped in a bright blue shawl and wore a very ugly black hat. In her brown-gloved hands she clasped an immense green reticule. Her blue eyes seemed anxious. She was trying to smile at us but she did not succeed.

'What a sight,' Kolia muttered into my ear, and ran away, leaving the three of us to do the honours. Nina said a few words of welcome in French but the lady from Dorpat obviously knew no French, and I was wicked enough to keep my own knowledge of German to myself.

'Katia, Katia,' pleaded Nina and Volodia in turn.

'Let us try Russian,' I whispered.

But the lady from Dorpat did not seem to understand any Russian either. I was unkind enough to keep up that comedy until Mademoiselle Berg was installed in her room and left in the care of Olga, an under-housemaid. Fat Dasha thought it degrading for her to look after a governess. 'I have my two young ladies to serve,' she said.

31

I must here explain that I was a little polyglot at the time. I dimly remember talking Danish with my mother, but, of course, all of it was nearly forgotten. At home, in Tver, it was either French or German with my father, and I had learned Russian from Agatha and other servants. I believe Cousin Sophie, who spoke it like a native, was slightly shocked at some of the idioms I used. Naturally, life at Trostnikovo taught me to speak it in the way my little cousins did.

Just before dinner was announced, I knew I must stammer my apologies to Mademoiselle Berg. But I need not have made any. As soon as I began speaking, she stooped, kissed me on both cheeks, called me her 'dear, dear child', and, in a word, looked as happy as though I had presented her with a birthday gift. Volodia and Nina seemed pleased enough, but Kolia, profiting by the absence of the grown-ups, teased me unmercifully all through the meal.

'Sausage-girl, sausage-girl.' He kept rocking in his chair. 'Who'd have thought we would have a sausage-girl for a cousin!'

Now, 'sausage-people', *kolbassniki*, meant Germans in Russian. Certainly, it was slang and Kolia should never have used it. I got furious.

'I am not a German—'

'You speak it,' he taunted me. 'Papa does not. And Cousin Sophie speaks it very badly.'

Poor Mademoiselle Berg! She understood nothing of it all except that her 'dear, dear child' and a vivacious black-eyed boy were obviously having a quarrel. Nor could I explain anything to her because Kolia kept repeating his contempt for all the Germans in the world.

In a word, it was a very difficult meal. Old Ivan's face remained impassive but we knew he disapproved. It was a relief to leave the dining-room, and I must confess that the over-sugared manner of Mademoiselle Berg whenever she spoke or looked at me, did not please me at all.

32

Poor woman! It was quite a time before we got used to her and came to love her—yes, even Kolia. And lovable she certainly was. She proved a good enough teacher, though I doubt if she knew the meaning of the word 'strictness'. A gentle, shy and rather lonely creature, she would blush deep scarlet whenever Cousin Sophie or any of the others addressed her. But she could certainly teach. What was more so far as we four were concerned—she could amuse us. The art of story-telling was inborn in her. Folk-lore, fairy-tales, stories from old German mythology and the great epics like the Nibelungen and Gudrun, Mademoiselle Berg was at home in them all. She opened an enchanting world to us from the very start of her life at Trostnikovo, and she proved as indefatigable as Cousin Sophie.

## 4 *The tragedy*

'Young ladies, it is time to get up,' Fat Dasha's loud voice rang in our room one Sunday morning in August. 'All the others are up—and I hear so many guests are coming.'

'Who are coming?' cried Nina and I together.

'Why, I don't rightly know—but Madame Lukanova and the children will be here for certain. The mistress's maid told me there was a letter from her last night.'

Nina leapt out of bed.

'Lili, Lili is coming! Oh, Katia, she is just wonderful! Dasha, shall I be allowed to wear my pink muslin today?'

'Why, yes, miss! The mistress said so.'

'And what shall I wear?' I asked, getting up in my turn.

'You, miss?' There was a hint of irony in Fat Dasha's voice. She looked after us both, but it was Nina who remained 'my young lady', and early enough I sensed a certain veiled insolence in Fat Dasha's manner to me. So now she said, 'You, miss?', pursed her mouth, and went on: 'Why, it is always the same frock for you on Sundays—the white one with the green pinafore.'

'Oh, Katia,' said Nina, whilst Fat Dasha knelt to lace up her little boots, 'I wish Cousin Sophie would have those sleeves altered. They are so ugly.'

At that very moment, Parasha, our thirteen-year-old schoolroom maid, came in, panting, a heavy jug of water in her hands. Her face was all swollen, her eyes were red, her blue print kerchief sat awry on her head. I had grown very fond of Parasha and often shared my sweets with her. That morning she looked as though she had been weeping for hours.

'Parasha, what have you been crying about?' I asked.

She put the jug down by the washstand, turned her face towards a corner and sobbed.

'Don't you howl so,' Fat Dasha admonished her. 'Why, Mademoiselle Berquovist might hear you, or the German lady. What would they think?'

Parasha's shoulders were shaking. Frightened and baffled, we showered questions at her. She wept on. At last Fat Dasha shook her head.

'Leave her be, young ladies. She might feel a bit better after a good cry. There is trouble indeed! Why, her only brother, Andrew, is being sent into the army tomorrow.'

'Andrew the carpenter?' exclaimed Nina and I together, and both of us remembered the scene once witnessed in the library.

Suddenly poor Parasha flung herself at Nina's feet.

'Miss Nina, Miss Nina, ask your father to pardon him. I beg you ... we'll all pray for you all our life. Miss Nina—'

Both of us were on the verge of tears when Mademoiselle Berg came in.

'Children, what has happened?' she asked in German.

Parasha at once scrambled to her feet and ran out of the room. Dasha whispered to us:

'Don't you tell anything to the German lady. Why, it might get to the master.'

I believe we invented some reason for Parasha's distress. Mademoiselle Berg, whose curiosity did not go very far, heard us rather indifferently and urged us to get dressed. On the way to breakfast, Nina and I decided that she would that very evening, when saying good night to Uncle Nicholas, ask for Andrew to be reprieved. Her father seldom, if ever, refused anything she asked of him.

'I shan't tell him till the evening,' said Nina. 'There will be all those guests. Mind, Katia, don't say a word to anyone.

Let it be a secret between us two.'

The whole family were already in the dining-room when we came in. Even Aunt Marie, exquisite in a cloud of pale blue tulle, sat at the table, drinking her coffee. When Uncle Nicholas began kissing Nina, she took his face between her hands and said rather solemnly:

'Dear, dear Papa, I have something very, very big to ask of you. But not now—in the evening.'

'I will remind you,' laughed Uncle Nicholas and he kissed her again.

Here the butler announced the carriage and the grown-ups left for church. I rather hoped to spend the morning with Nina, but she vanished, and Kolia lured me into the oak coppice at the back of the kitchen-gardens.

'You just wait, Katia,' he said quite seriously. 'As soon as that dreadful French doll arrives, Nina won't have a moment for you.'

'What French doll?'

'Why, Lili Lukanova. She and her brother make me sick. They were here just before your arrival, and there was Nina running after Lili all day long.'

Something like jealousy crept into my thoughts.

'Are they coming for long?' I asked rather anxiously.

'I can't tell. Last time they stayed for ages. Now Nina will be running here, there and everywhere. Br-br-br,' and Kolia made a face.

'Nina is not like that,' I said stoutly.

'Isn't she? Our Aunt Lena once called her a weathercock,' he retorted.

It was on the tip of my tongue to tell him that his sister and I shared a tremendous secret no Lili Lukanova would ever know anything about, but I checked myself in time, and we raced each other to the brook at the end of the oak coppice.

It must have been some special Sunday because so many guests came to dine at Trostnikovo that day. When Kolia and I got back to the house, the Lukanov family had already arrived. The mother, a small, plump woman, dressed as if for a ball, her blonde hair arranged in ringlets *à l'anglaise*, spoke nothing but French. Her voice rang languid, she looked as though people in the room were not quite good enough for her, and I disliked the way she kept stroking her right hand with her left. Her daughter, Lili, was a smaller edition of the mother, and when I saw Nina rush towards her, I could not but remember Kolia's words.

Lili Lukanova was about a year older than Nina. Very fair, with enormous grey eyes, very small hands and feet, she did look like a doll. Her pink silk dress all ruffles and flounces, she curtseyed to everybody she met, spoke very quietly, never started any conversation but only answered questions, and studiedly added 'Madame, Monsieur, Mademoiselle' to every answer she made. I suppose she was what some fond mothers called an exemplary child—so impeccably did she behave, but her clothes, her coiffure and mannerisms made me loathe her at sight. Nina and she sat down together in a corner, Nina chattering like a proverbial magpie, 'the French doll' smiling waxenly and putting in an occasional remark. For the life of me I could not understand what Nina saw in her.

Cousin Sophie presented me to Madame Lukanova. My curtsy was anything but graceful. She looked at me rather distantly and drawled in French:

'Oh, how very pale is the little one.'

Lili shook hands as ceremoniously as though we were both grown-up society women and at once turned to Nina, whose face was positively radiant. I must say I did not feel particularly happy that day.

I found Kolia seated alone in a corner and I shared his chair.

'Well,' he winked at me, 'isn't she just a beastly dressed-up doll?'

I nodded.

'I wish their place were not so near to Trostnikovo,' Kolia went on, 'then we would never have to meet them. Thank goodness, though, they are seldom in the country. And the brother is even worse than the sister. I can't stick him. He stinks of scent, for one thing. Papa would fly into a temper if Volodia and I put such stuff on our hair. There he is—stepping out. Look, Katia.'

I turned my head and saw our Volodia modestly dressed in a grey linen blouse and pale blue pantaloons, and by his side a boy of about twelve, his blond, carefully curled hair falling down on his shoulders. I had never seen such a boy in my life. He wore a dark blue cloth coat with gilt buttons, a snow-white collar covering his shoulders, white velvet breeches, prunelle shoes and gaiters. He did not walk—he stepped out. I wished I might giggle. And yet I admired him.

'Here you are, tomboy,' he said to Kolia, who shook hands in most unpromising silence. Misha Lukanov looked at me.

'That is Katia,' Volodia introduced us. 'She is just like our sister.'

Misha made me a little bow and strutted on.

'Well,' said Kolia, 'what did I tell you?'

No, it was not a very happy day for me. Kolia soon vanished and I knew he had run off to the stables, there to have a good talk with his old friend, Ermila, the head coachman. Nina and Lili seemed glued together on a tiny sofa in one of the drawing-rooms. Volodia was trying to entertain Misha. There were no other children, and I sat on the steps of the terrace all by myself. From time to time I remembered 'the secret' and it made me feel a little less miserable.

After a light luncheon which we children had in a small room away from all the other guests, Nina and Volodia suggested a walk in the park. Even then Misha insisted on ceremony. He offered his arm to Nina and told Volodia to take Lili. I certainly did not take Kolia's arm. We two just followed in the rear.

Misha did not seem to take much notice of the park. He held forth mostly about Paris and other foreign resorts. I listened with interest—much though I disliked him. We reached a clearing, made for a bench, and Misha said to Nina:

'I suppose you were simply dying of boredom here. Always the same people and the same things to do. I suppose you must have got sick even of your garden.'

But, to my great pleasure, that was too much for Nina.

'Stop it, Misha! What has happened to you?' she broke in. 'You have become such an important little boy and you talk nonsense. Why, the last time you came, you told us our garden was something out of a fairy-tale.'

'My dear Nina,' said Misha composedly. 'It was some time ago—and Lili and I were such children then. Now that we have seen so many marvels, we think most of what we used to see before is rubbish.'

'Ah, I suppose we are rubbish,' said Volodia, who did not seem at all at ease with 'the French doll', who sat with a pink silk parasol over her head.

'Of course not. Lili and I would never be brought here if your house were not *comme il faut*. But there is just one thing I don't like here—'

'And what is it?' asked Nina and Volodia together, and I saw Kolia make one of his hideous faces at no one in particular.

'Well,' drawled that detestable boy, 'you are dressed so badly. Nina in a pink muslin probably made by some sewing-maid at home—'

Nina looked angry.

'Mama had that dress made for me at Kursk by the very best dressmaker,' she retorted.

'Well, all right,' and here Misha tugged at my sleeve. 'Surely such sleeves went out of fashion ages ago ... Volodia in a grey blouse and pantaloons, and Kolia in a white blouse ...'

Kolia whistled. Volodia looked hurt. I almost wept because I knew that my sleeves were ugly. Nina said very little but she looked cross. On the way back she walked with Lili and I felt wickedly pleased not to hear so much chatter.

'Kolia was wrong,' I kept thinking. 'Nina is not a weathercock and these dreadful people won't stay here for ever.'

And my misery vanished altogether when, as we got nearer to the house, Nina slipped her hand out of Lili's and turned to whisper to me:

'You have not forgotten "the secret", Katia?'

'No, no,' I assured her fervently.

'And you haven't mentioned it to anyone?'

I shook my head.

After dinner, which we again had by ourselves, all the guests came out on the terrace for coffee. We five settled down on the steps, and I noticed that Misha's oratory had by now dwindled down to an occasional harmless remark.

The weather was simply magnificent. Men got out their pipes. All around us were loud voices and laughter, and suddenly we heard Uncle Nicholas say loudly:

'Now, my friends, what are we going to do in the afternoon?'

At once my little cousins leapt to their feet and begged to go to Dnieprovka to fish.

'Splendid,' said their father and beckoned to the butler. 'Ivan, tell them to get the brake ready in about an hour. The roans—'

At that moment a loud shot rang out just behind the garden, towards the stables. Its echo died away in the park. Everybody screamed. I scrambled to my feet and ran to Mademoiselle Berg. I was trembling from head to foot.

'What was that?' asked Uncle Nicholas, staring at the butler, whose face turned a chalky white.

'I don't know, sir. Let me find out,' and he ran down the steps towards a little gate leading into the courtyard.

On the terrace nobody moved or spoke. From a distance we heard the thumping of several feet, someone's shriek, someone's wild howl. Then suddenly all was still again, and the old butler came back.

'Sir, Andrew the carpenter has shot himself.'

The words fell into the briefest of all brief silences. Nina's shriek startled us.

'Papa! Papa!' She rushed to Uncle Nicholas. 'What have I done? It is my fault.... I meant to say in the evening... in the evening. What have I done?'

Uncle Nicholas picked her up in his arms and ran into the house. Aunt Marie followed them, her face wet with tears. I hid my head in Mademoiselle Berg's lap and wept and wept.

'What in the world has happened?' asked Madame Lukanova, and Cousin Sophie answered coldly:

'I could not really tell you. I suppose the child got frightened.'

'And there is your own little girl, crying her eyes out.'

Cousin Sophie ran up to me.

'Katia, Katia!'

'I am so sorry—for poor Parasha—' I muttered through my tears. 'Mamma, she begged Nina—'

'Tell me later, dearest,' Cousin Sophie interrupted and led me away from the terrace.

In the night poor Nina was so ill that they had to send for the doctor. The Lukanova family left in the morning, the mother being anxious lest her darlings were to fall ill in their turn. Nina was ill for some days. She and I never spoke of the tragedy. I suppose she could not bear to talk of it and I was strictly forbidden to mention it. So, I now suppose, was Fat Dasha. Andrew's sister, Parasha, no longer came into the house, and we children were told that he had shot him-self by accident.

Did we believe it? I think we did because our minds just could not conceive that Uncle Nicholas, Aunt Marie, or

Cousin Sophie were capable of telling us a lie. And yet I do remember that—however fond I was of Uncle Nicholas, I sometimes felt not at my ease with him. It seemed to me that even an accident would never have happened unless *he* had done something to bring it about. My thoughts were vague and confused. I was far too small to know anything about serfdom and its horrors, and, once Nina recovered and our ordinary busy life went on as usual, we forgot to think about Andrew the carpenter. Yet something must have stayed in the memory because the horror had bitten really deep.

## 5 *Was there a plum-tree in the Garden of Eden?*

I believe it was in the autumn of my second year at Trostnikovo that Aunt Marie had news of her mother's illness at
Kiev and decided to go there and stay till Christmas. Uncle
Nicholas left us at the same time for a month's tour of his
estates in the Provinces of Ryazan and Tula. Very few
visitors came to the house during their absence, and we four
worked hard at our lessons.

How clearly do I remember the fruit harvest of that year
because of a storm breaking over my little head!

The orchards at Trostnikovo were so immense that it
needed a crowd of men and women and even children to
gather the fruit. Early at dawn, they came, armed with
baskets and trugs of all shapes and sizes, and they never
stopped singing as they worked. Wherever we went, we saw
mounds of red-cheeked and green-veined apples, pale golden
pears and enormous plums of all shades from darkest purple
to palest yellow. Fine weather held and the air was cloyingly
fragrant. Every day, when out in the gardens, we were allowed
to eat one pear and two plums each. Just two plums! And
oh, I was a rather greedy little girl and I preferred plums
to any other fruit. I could quite easily have eaten a whole
dozen at a sitting. I once seriously said to the others that
when I was grown up I would have neither soup nor meat
for my dinner—but plums only.

It so happened that one day our dear Monsieur Filipov
was coming to dinner. He was a wealthy neighbour whose
sole purpose in life seemed to be to amuse the children he
knew. We were very fond of him. The parties he gave at his

huge place across the river were always memorable occasions.

The morning lessons were over. Cousin Sophie was so pleased with me that day that she kissed me several times and sent me straight into the garden. I ran into Volodia in a passage.

'Oh, Katia,' he cried, licking his lips, 'what a dessert we are going to have today! Peaches, grapes, pears, plums, melon, rose jam and goodness only knows what else.'

'Have you seen it?'

'Oh yes. Come and I'll show you.' He seized me by the hand and we ran towards the big drawing-room. There, a big porcelain basket, filled with most artistically arranged fruit, stood in the middle of a round table. We ran up, admired and sniffed rather hungrily. At that moment a footman came in to tell Volodia that his tutor was expecting him.

'What a bore,' he sighed, and whispered to me: 'Try one of the plums. Nobody will find out—there's such a lot of them.'

'Never,' I retorted and ran through the French window into the rose-garden. Quite honestly I tried not to think about the fruit. For one thing, we were strictly forbidden to eat between meals.

But soon enough I felt I had had enough of the roses. I knew that Nina was doing her French with Cousin Sophie; Volodia had gone to his tutor and I had no idea of Kolia's whereabouts. I turned towards the window. The drawing-room was temptingly empty. The porcelain basket drew me on and on, its fragrant contents something of a work of art, but I was not thinking of that. My eyes were riveted on one particular corner where some big golden plums lay cradled in among black grapes. I tiptoed to the table, carefully pulled out three of the biggest plums, dropped them into the pocket of my pinafore, flew back into the garden, and ate them hurriedly, but taking care not to let the roseate juice stain my little white muslin cape. Having tossed the stones into a rose-bush, I hesitated. What were three plums after all? I went back to the drawing-room.

My hand was already stretched out when I heard steps outside a door to the left. I leapt away from the table and threw myself on the floor, pretending to be engrossed in the pattern of the carpet.

Cousin Sophie came in.

'What? All by yourself, dearest?'

I jumped to my feet.

'The sun is so hot, Mamma, and Volodia was here a few minutes ago, but his tutor wanted him. Mamma, are we going to read *Robinson Crusoe* this evening?'

'Of course, of course,' she replied and made straight for the table, and my heart thudded when I heard her say, 'How very odd! There is hardly a plum to be seen in that corner.'

She spoke with her back to me. At that moment I could not have borne to meet her eyes. Here the old butler came in.

'You rang, Madam?'

'Yes, Ivan.' Cousin Sophie's voice was severe. 'Do you know if Mirza or any other page-boy has been here?'

'There has been nobody here, Madam, except Master Volodia and your little lady.'

Cousin Sophie turned to me. My ears were burning.

'Please take the fruit into the dining-room,' she said to the butler. She waited for him to leave the room, sat down in the nearest armchair, and asked, her voice studiedly quiet:

'Katia, could it be you?'

I stood rooted, head bent, the taste of the last plum still on my tongue.

'Look at me.'

I raised my head. Cousin Sophie's face was not angry but so sad that I rushed towards her, buried my burning face in her lap, and burst into tears.

'My dearest child, you could not have forgotten the eighth commandment. You must know what you have done.'

'Mamma, I'll never, never do it again,' I sobbed, 'I am so sorry. Please don't tell the others—I am so ashamed.'

'How could I speak of it to anyone? Your shame is also mine. My adopted daughter—discovered stealing plums! Hadn't I found you in this room, I would have blamed Mirza. I could never have believed it of you.'

'Volodia,' I stammered through my tears, 'said that nobody would ever know—'

'Nobody?' echoed my adopted mother. 'And what about God?'

I said nothing and sobbed all the harder. Her voice went on, very sad and gentle:

'I know I am more strict with you than with any of the other children, but they don't belong to me. You do. You are dearer to me than anyone else in the world. I am doing my utmost to have you brought up as an honest, truthful girl, and you are truthful. You may tell a fib one moment and the next your deep shame betrays you. I say again I would never have believed it of you. Now, dearest child, dry your eyes. I want you to choose. Either today during dessert you make a public admission of your theft, or when, in the future, something very pleasant should come your way, I will refuse to let you have it. Which is it to be?'

I thought very hard. The future seemed rather reassuringly remote. The prospect of an immediate humiliation scared me beyond words. I chose the second alternative and saw that Cousin Sophie was pleased with my choice.

She sent me upstairs to get my face washed. The sight of my swollen eyes made Fat Dasha pelt me with questions, and I added to the day's transgression by telling her that I had fallen rather awkwardly when jumping off the terrace steps. The theft of the plums remained a secret between Cousin Sophie and myself.

'And what about God?' she had asked during those painful moments in the drawing-room.

We children were hardly ever taken to church. I cannot

remember any bishops or other clerics visiting Trostnikovo, nor were any itinerant monks, nuns, or lay pilgrims ever welcomed by Cousin Nicholas. I cannot answer for him or for Aunt Marie, but my adopted mother certainly lived her religion. Both by precept and by her own example, she taught me to speak the truth, to keep my temper, to be conscientious at lessons—not out of fear of any punishment but for the love of God. We four said our morning and evening prayers together—in three languages. 'Our Father' and a short prayer to the Holy Spirit were the only formal pieces in Old Slavonic that we knew. All the others were composed for us in French by Cousin Sophie, and Mademoiselle Berg added her German prayer to the rest. We knew all the Bible stories and enjoyed them. We also knew a few Psalms in French and German, and I possessed a Danish New Testament, once belonging to my own mother. Cousin Sophie never taught me any theology proper, but she enabled me to see God as a person whose relationship to me was very real.

All of it formed part of our daily pattern—something as real as our hands and feet. We did not go about telling one another that we all had ten toes and ten fingers each. Much in the same way we did not talk piety. When I grew up, I realized that was not the Russian way, but it was a good way.

Days passed, and there was I—left with a solemn promise which I could not mention even to Nina from whom I had never before had a secret.

About a fortnight later, on a perfect September morning, we were having our German lessons with Mademoiselle Berg. I was sitting next to Kolia and suddenly he kicked my legs so hard that I dropped my pen. I stared at a huge blot of ink in the middle of the page. My copybooks were usually in a sorry state, smudged and stained all over, but this was worse than ever—and not my fault either. Here Kolia kicked me again.

'Stop,' I hissed at him. 'Look what you have done!'

He kicked me for the third time. I lost my temper and my elbow hit him hard in the ribs. He lost no time in hitting me in return.

'Children, children!' Our poor governess shook her head at us.

'Mademoiselle Berg, Kolia has been kicking me,' I cried.

'Then come to my end of the table,' she said. 'Kolia, for shame!'

I pushed my copybook down the table, got up and, bending, scratched right across the beautifully written page of Kolia's copybook. I must here explain that his penmanship stood very high. We were never praised publicly but we all knew that the grown-ups were rather proud of Kolia's writing.

And now I had ruined a whole page of it. Furious, he jumped to his feet, grabbed my miserable copybook and poured ink all over it. I howled. He shouted. Poor Mademoiselle Berg kept telling us to be quiet. We did not listen to her. Nina added to the tumult by shrieking that it was all Kolia's fault. Volodia screamed that I was to blame. The pandemonium reached its peak when suddenly the old butler opened the door. He brought a letter for Nina. Fists raised, faces flushed, we all stopped shouting at once.

'From Papa, from Papa?' cried the boys together.

Nina glanced at the signature and smiled.

'Not from Papa. I think it is a surprise,' and she ran out of the room in search of Cousin Sophie. The quarrel instantly forgotten, the boys and I followed her.

It took us quite a time to find my adopted mother. At last we came on her in a wing where she was inspecting the rooms prepared for Uncle Nicholas's niece, Nastia Ratassova, whom I had not yet met, but of whom I had heard much from my little cousins, who adored her. Nastia, recently left an orphan, was coming for some months' visit.

'Cousin Sophie, Cousin Sophie,' cried Nina, brandishing

her letter, 'I have just heard from Monsieur Filipov. Please read it to us. I can't make it out.'

Cousin Sophie stopped arranging a few oddments on the dressing-table and smiled at our eager faces. Fortunately, it did not occur to her to ask whether we had finished our German lesson.

'Ah, a letter from Monsieur Filipov? I have been expecting it, Nina.'

We heard that we were being invited to dinner the very next Sunday. 'And after dinner,' wrote the kind old man, 'we will take the boat down the river. Later, I thought we might have a mushroom hunt in the wood and tea with "surprises" in the oak coppice. And I have arranged for fireworks at the end.'

It was five treats in one! Monsieur Filipov's tea with 'surprises' meant, as we knew by pleasant experience, most temptingly wrapped little parcels for each of us. I greatly cherished a box of coloured crayons which had once fallen to my share. And fireworks at the end . . .

We shouted 'Hurrah' at the very top of our voices and began leaping and dancing about the room.

'Shall I wear the white muslin with the new blue sash?' asked Nina, who had inherited her mother's fondness for clothes.

'Oh yes,' replied Cousin Sophie.

'And wouldn't it be nice if Katia wore hers, too?' Nina went on.

'We shall see, we shall see.' Cousin Sophie spoke without looking at me, and Volodia broke in:

'I would like to wear my new blue coat with the bronze buttons, Cousin Sophie.'

Cousin Sophie shook her head very decisively.

'Certainly not. You and Kolia had best wear linen blouses. Much better for boating and for running about in the wood. That new coat of yours, Volodia, would be ruined at once.'

'But I do want to wear it. What is the good of having a smart coat if I am never allowed to wear it?' whimpered Volodia and he started bitsing his thumb-nail.

'You will be left at home if you go on biting your nails,' Cousin Sophie told him.

'Then Kolia should not go either. He is always up to mischief. Look what he did this morning. He and Katia—'

'Volodia,' Nina stamped her little foot, 'stop at once, will you? How often has Papa punished you for telling tales?'

A small pause followed. Cousin Sophie, no longer smiling, looked first at me and then at Kolia. I did not know what to say when Kolia burst out:

'Cousin Sophie, please let me tell you all about it. It was all my fault. I kicked Katia's leg under the table. I did, and her pen fell and made a frightful mess of a page, and she got angry and kicked me back—and that was all—' he panted.

I could have fallen on his neck for gratitude. Cousin Sophie loathed tale-telling. She took no notice whatever either of Volodia's words or of Kolia's artless defence.

'I am very busy, children. All of you go into the garden. Nina, tell someone to lay the table under the limes. It is such a lovely day—we had better dine out of doors.'

It was a Saturday. We had no lessons that afternoon and spent hours in discussing the treat in store. Nina and I decided we would wear stout shoes for greater comfort during the mushroom hunt, and I remembered that I must not eat apricots because they disagreed with me. We all four were extremely curious about 'the surprises'. Nina hoped for a small doll, Volodia for a book, Kolia for a whistle, and I dreamt about a painted wooden apple, with needles and cottons inside. Cousin Sophie came in whilst we were having supper. Tomorrow's theme engaged us all through the meal.

All through that day her manner to me was perfectly ordinary. Of course, I had not forgotten my promise. But I kept saying, 'This is not just "something pleasant" as she had said. This is five pleasures rolled into one.' So I kept saying to myself, but I was such a little coward that I just did not dare to come up to her and say—'Mamma, could my promise be kept some time later on?' I think I rather expected her to say something. But she did not. Even when kissing me good night after prayers, she said nothing at all.

The morning broke, beautifully sunny, and Fat Dasha came to call us.

'Miss Katia,' she said almost at once, 'I have had no orders about your dress today. What are you going to wear?'

My heart nearly missed a beat. Nina answered for me: 'Why, the white muslin—just as I am.'

'Miss Katia's white muslin is still in the chest,' replied Fat Dasha, and I looked across the room.

'The key is in the lock, Dasha,' I said.

'So it is.' Fat Dasha waddled across and lifted the lid. There lay my little white muslin, all newly ironed, the broad blue sash folded on top of it. I sighed in relief as Dasha began doing my hair.

Presently it was time to dress. Cousin Sophie came into the room. She smiled at Nina and took no notice of me. I got into my little stays as best I could and began struggling with the hooks, but I could not manage much on my own. Whenever I asked Fat Dasha to help me, Cousin Sophie at once told her to do something for Nina, who, when ready, ran off to join her brothers. Cousin Sophie moved to the door, telling Dasha to send word to the coachman to have the carriage by the door in ten minutes.

'I have not dressed your little lady yet, Madam,' mumbled Fat Dasha.

'Do what you are told,' Cousin Sophie said severely and left the room.

And I was left alone. I heard the carriage come to the front door. I heard someone shouting about a parasol. I could not leave the room—my frock unlaced, my hair undressed, the boots falling off my feet. I shouted, 'Dasha, Dasha, Olga, Olga—' But nobody answered and nobody came. . . .

## 6 *Such a happy winter . . .*

One day in late autumn a note came from Uncle Nicholas announcing that he and his niece, Nastia, would be with us in a few days. I had been expecting her eagerly enough— but with something like anxiety in a corner of my mind. The children were tireless in singing her praises. Nastia, it appeared, would join us in all our games, she could row like a boy, and was particularly good with the ball. I heard that she would certainly make new dresses for our dolls, teach us new dancing-steps and always be willing to tell us stories in the evening.

I listened. I felt slightly afraid of an intrusion. Eighteen months of close companionship with my three cousins made me dislike the very thought of anyone else joining our little circle. Step by step, the little demon of jealousy began occupying my thoughts. Nina was as near to me as a sister. Suppose that Nastia—for all that she was much older than either of us—should step in and rob me of some of that friendship? I tried not to think of it too much. I mentioned it to nobody, not even to Cousin Sophie.

And what a little fool I was! Nastia, aged about nineteen, very pretty, her eyes the colour of harebells, proved a friend from the very first day. Indeed it was not very long before it seemed as though her heart, so far as we children were concerned, was divided into four scrupulously equal parts. And what fun she was! She taught us the quadrille just then coming into fashion, and gypsy songs, and she brought wooden jigsaw puzzles from Moscow, something we had never seen before. I remember there was a big one representing the map of Europe, and I came to like it much more than any geography textbook. Our hours of leisure became noisier and more merry than ever before, and Cousin Sophie, who warmly approved of Nastia, had a little more time for her correspondence and articles.

And then winter was upon us, and it proved an exceptionally hard one. For all our Spartan upbringing, there were days when we must keep indoors—so blinding the blizzard, so cruel the wind. Stoves in all the rooms would be stoked twice and sometimes three times a day, and all the windows had thick double frames fixed to them. Daylight went before our three o'clock dinner and we got up by candle-light. Except for the weekly bath, we were not allowed hot water for washing. The huge jugs brought in by Fat Dasha and Olga contained something not far removed from ice. Yet I cannot remember anyone getting chilblains. The only one who would complain was poor Volodia, but we did not take much notice of him.

Yet blizzards did not happen every day, and one of the amusements offered by winter was driving in an open sledge. The pleasure of a drive came but three or four times during the summer when we went to some party in the neighbourhood. Now we enjoyed a sledge drive as many times a week if the weather allowed it. Wrapped in shawls and furs from head to foot, with a bearskin rug covering us, we would fly across the long avenue, past the park, along the river bank, Nina and I holding our small ermine muffs against our faces. How good it was! The sharp smell of snow, the sunlight glinting over the trees, sparks flying off the horses' hoofs, the wide river carpeted with gleaming ice, and the low broad sledge going ever faster and faster. Nina and I held our breath. . . .

In the great courtyard the snow was swept into huge mounds at the four corners, and there we could run about, snowballing one another for all we were worth. Uncle Nicholas had a huge snow mountain built on a lawn. A dozen or so of wooden steps led up to the top, and we four and Nastia, too, had small sledges made for us at the carpenter's shop. The sledge hour was usually after morning lessons, and it became so precious that I would exert myself even with the hateful 'sums' so as not to be deprived of that pleasure. One Sunday Uncle Nicholas and Nastia helped us to make a snowman in front of the terrace. Two small coals for eyes, a pipe thrust into the mouth, and a tricorne made of thick blue paper with a panache of straw and hay, made our snow gentleman most attractive, and we at once christened him *Graf Morozov*, i.e. 'Count Frost'.

Kolia and I had far less orthodox amusements. He would lure me towards an enormous snowdrift in some remote corner of the courtyard or the stable-yard, and help me to climb it. Usually, I got stuck half-way up. I would try to struggle out of the soft clinging snow, get deeper and deeper into it, and at last, pushed and pulled by Kolia, roll down to the bottom, snow flecking my eyelashes and mouth and my brown coat and boots most beautifully white. Mademoiselle Berg saw me tumble one day and she was horrified.

'My dear child, you should never play such rough games. You are not a boy. Why, even your gloves are wet through.'

'Don't you listen to her,' Kolia said later. 'Papa always says that a good wetting has never hurt anyone yet.'

It certainly did not hurt any of us. We were dressed warmly enough when we went out of doors, but nobody made any fuss when we came back, our stockings soaked up to the knee. Our boots and hose pulled off, we had our feet and legs rubbed with warm red wine, and not one of us ever caught a cold.

But the greatest star in our wintry sky shone indoors, and it shone seldom enough, its splendour gaining from the rarity of its appearances. It was the dolls' theatre managed by Cousin Sophie. She wrote all the pieces herself, and they were written in Russian for the benefit of the household who, beginning with the old butler and ending with the youngest maid in the kitchens, were always invited to the performance.

It was always held on Saturday evenings, a reward for a whole week of good behaviour and hard study of us four.

'Well, children, you are going to see a play this evening,' said Cousin Sophie one day in December when lunch was over. She left the room before our shouts of joy deafened her completely.

What a trial was the dinner that day! We were all so excited, we fairly burst with it, and at table we could not talk. We were only allowed to answer questions asked by the grown-ups.

It had taken me quite a time to get used to that particular rule at Trostnikovo. Ivan and two or three footmen were waiting at table. We never helped ourselves but waited for one of the men to put the food on our plates. Not all the dishes came our way but, if something specially appetizing was being served, it was just fatal to ask for it. Ivan would be given an immediate sign to pass the culprit by. Once I had a most unfortunate experience of a different kind. Real gluttony was not one of my faults, but I did like good things. It was a Sunday and a very special raspberry pudding, served with a thick cream sauce, was offered to us. Ivan stopped near my chair and started by putting some of the sauce on my plate. He was rather slow. Impatient, I seized the spoon and began eating the sauce. At once I heard Cousin Sophie's voice:

'Ivan, Miss Katia has had enough. Please give her no more.'

And there was the butler offering the dish to Mademoiselle Berg and nothing but two spoonfuls of the sauce on my plate. Volodia got into different trouble often enough. He would crumble his bread and scatter it all round his plate once the soup was finished. Just before the sweet, a footman would be told to scoop up all the crumbs and put them on Volodia's pudding plate. Tears at table did not particularly help us.

That Saturday dinner seemed to last for ages. I felt so excited about the dolls' theatre that I kept up a silent monologue with my spoon, knife and fork.

After an eternity of waiting, the clocks struck six, and we heard the longed-for bell. The great ballroom was dark except for two slim candles burning behind a partition. Aunt Marie, Mademoiselle Berg, Nastia and we four sat in the first row. A big table was placed at one end of the room and some contraption stood on it—screened by a long curtain. Another bell rang as soon as the audience came in, and the curtain parted in two. Behind was a forest, and we saw a hunting scene from the Middle Ages. There were knights, their ladies, a huntsman and a few pages, all cut out of black paper. The scenery must have been made of some transparent material—with a few candles burning backstage so that every tree could be seen quite clearly. Cousin Sophie, whom we could not see, moved the dolls up and down the stage by means of most cunningly contrived wires. She spoke all the lines, too, altering her voice very convincingly. One of the ladies having been lost in the forest, the rest were looking for her. Presently, she was found. Then a page was missing. When he reappeared, he said he had come on a great treasure somewhere far away in the forest. Should they ride and look at it? 'No, no,' said one of the knights, 'the treasure can wait. We have come to hunt the boar—' and the curtains drew together again.

It was all very simple but oh, we drank in every word, and during the interval, I glowed with pride at the comments of the audience. Cousin Sophie's triumph was my own. I felt there was just nobody in the world as clever as she. I clapped until I could clap no more, and Aunt Marie smiled, and said:

'Well, kitten, perhaps some day you may be as clever as Mamma is.'

'Never, never, Aunt Marie. Nobody could ever be as clever

as she is.'

The curtains parted and we saw the boar. He looked terrific. The ladies were gone. Had they ridden to look for the treasure, we wondered. A knight was unsaddled. He seemed in such danger that we held our breath. But another man engaged the boar's attention. A minute, and he, too, lay on the ground and the boar was about to leap, when a young page, brandishing a dagger, ran to the rescue. Down went the boar, and all the knights rode closer and closer. Hunt servants dragged the boar away, and the page was rewarded for his bravery by the gift of a gold necklace from the treasure he had found.

As soon as Cousin Sophie had been congratulated by all the others, I rushed at her.

'Mamma, Mamma, it was wonderful, just wonderful. I can't thank you enough.'

Then, all too suddenly, Christmas was round the corner. The tree, the presents, and finally, the possible arrival of my cousins' uncle, Aunt Marie's brother, these three themes occupied our spare moments. An officer in some guards regiment, he had not been at Trostnikovo for more than two years because of some trouble in the Caucasus, so we were told. Nina called him 'the most handsome man in the world' and said that he and Nastia were very fond of each other. Kolia dismissed all of it as 'girls' rubbish' and informed me that Uncle Basil was the best horseman in the regiment.

Christmas Eve came. A severe frost had begun in the early morning. It was such a clear evening that you could see all the stars. Dinner finished, we were sent upstairs and told we must remain there until someone came to call us. We knew the reason perfectly well. Such a bustle was going on below, and the tree was being decorated in the ballroom.

We had hardly finished tea when Nastia ran in. She looked lovelier than ever in a deeply flounced dress of pale pink tulle. She filled the room with the fragrance of pine-needles so that we guessed she had been in the ballroom. She held a very long stick in her hands.

'Off with you all to the Blue Room,' she commanded. 'But first get out your handkerchiefs and tie them over your eyes. Get hold of the stick and I'll bring you downstairs in safety.'

How we laughed bandaging one another's eyes. We knew quite well that we would have to pass the ballroom doors on our way to the Blue Room. We came down the stairs rather carefully. Then we ran. Footsteps and voices rang on every side. We seemed to be surrounded by people hurrying about on some very mysterious business. But we saw nothing at all.

Once in the Blue Room, Nastia cried:

'Off with the handkerchiefs! Stay here and please behave!'

We arranged ourselves comfortably on one of the big sofas, and Nina sighed:

'I do wish I knew what Mamma is going to give me.'

'A *sámovar*, I think,' Volodia said.

'How in the world do you know?'

'Well, the day one of the bailiffs was sent to Kursk, I heard Cousin Sophie say to Mamma, "Tell them not to buy a big one. The children might scald themselves." '

'I suppose you eavesdropped—as usual,' Kolia whistled. Volodia blushed scarlet.

'I did not,' he began indignantly, but it was not the hour for a quarrel. Kolia turned away and winked at me.

'I know one present Katia is going to get. I heard from Papa, but he made me promise not to tell.'

'Kolia, dearest,' said I, my arm about his neck, 'please, is it something big or small?'

'Well, middling.'

'Useful, or just nice?'

'Oh, very, very nice.'

'To play with, or to eat?'

'I can't tell you.'

'Have I ever said I would like to have it?'

Kolia knit his black eyebrows.

'I think you once said that you would have liked to see her.'

'See her?' Nina and I cried together. 'Goodness, is it something alive?'

Kolia laughed, and shook his head.

'I can't tell you any more.'

I went on wheedling and wheedling, but the boy kept shaking his head.

'You will know soon enough,' was all he said.

'I wonder if Uncle Basil will come today,' said Nina. 'Poor darling Nastia will be so disappointed if he does not.'

'Quiet all of you,' Kolia shouted suddenly and he jumped on to the broad window-sill. 'I hear a bell—'

We followed him to the window-sill. The great courtyard was well lit with innumerable torches, and we saw men running towards the main gates and heard the none too distant jingle of bells. In a few moments a hooded *tróyka* clattered into the courtyard.

'It is Uncle Basil,' shrieked Kolia. 'Those are his greys and it is his batman on the box.'

Almost at once the door of an adjoining room was thrown open and Uncle Nicholas called out:

'Come along, children! Uncle Basil has arrived.'

My cousins ran, and I followed them. The hall was crowded with domestics. I halted near a doorway and saw a slim, very handsome officer, his overcoat flecked with snow, run up and kiss Aunt Marie.

'Welcome! Certainly better late than never, Basil,' she said.

'I did say I would try to get leave for Christmas,' he laughed and turned to greet the others. 'Cousin Sophie.' He stooped to kiss her hand, and then he saw Nastia, whose eyes were starry. 'And you here, too—and the children! Well, dears—'

Then came the turn of what visitors were staying in the house and of the domestics. Uncle Basil was particularly tender with old Nannie Lizbeth, who had nursed him. I saw Aunt Marie and Nastia stand arm in arm, and my three little cousins clinging to their uncle wherever he moved, and there was Uncle Nicholas shouting various orders to the butler and the footmen. I stood where I was, and for the very first time since leaving my father's house, I felt alone, shy, an outsider, having no right to share in an intimate family pleasure. I still kept near that doorway. If Cousin Sophie were near, I would have run to her, but, having greeted Uncle Basil, she seemed to have vanished out of the hall. My mouth was perilously near trembling when I heard her voice:

'Katia, Katia, where are you? I have been looking for you.' The horrified feeling completely gone, I hurried towards her.

'Basil, here is my little daughter.'

'May I kiss you? And you will call me "Uncle", won't you?' He stooped, his moustache tickling my cheek. Utterly embarrassed, I dropped him a curtsy—to everybody's amusement.

Poor Uncle Basil must have needed his hot tea, but he was not given much time to enjoy it. Several bells rang at once, the great doors of the ballroom were flung open. Kolia's bony fingers squeezing my hand, I found myself entering an enchanted kingdom.

In the middle of the ballroom stood an enormous tree—all mantled with light. Whole necklaces of tiny candles were burning from the top fronds right down to the bottom. Kolia ran away. I stumbled against Cousin Sophie, thrust my hand into hers, and walked round and round the tree, unable to take in all the delights it offered. Multicoloured candles, thin, curvy streamers of silver tinfoil flung from branch to branch, the gleaming gilt star at the very top, tiny red apples and golden pears, gilt walnuts, miniature baskets, covered with red and pink paper and filled with sweets, chocolate dolls, fiddles and fishes wrapped in gold and silver, birds and beasts of white and pink sugar, gingerbread hearts studded with tiny fellow sweets—and all of it simply drowned in light.

I just had no words. The others were already shouting with delight at their presents. Very dimly did I see them—Kolia astride a rocking-horse. Nina with her tiny real *sámovar* and a pretty tea-service, Volodia and his big box of colours. I saw them and I did not see them. I was lost in rapture, until Aunt Marie laid a hand on my shoulder.

'Kitten, you have not had your presents yet. Look what I got for you at Kiev.'

I turned, saw, gasped, and clapped my hands. There stood an exquisite doll in gleaming armour and a brief skirt of red velvet. She wore a helmet and held an embroidered banner in one hand.

'Joan of Arc,' I cried, and heard Kolia's excited voice:
'What did I tell you? What did I tell you? Didn't you say how much you wished you could have met her?'

And I remembered one day after Cousin Sophie had told us the story of Joan of Arc, I had felt so carried away that I could not help exclaiming, 'Oh, how I wish I could have seen her.'

I had no words left to thank Aunt Marie. A beautiful Russian history in pictures, two German story-books, and a leather workbox were among my other presents. It was not the end, however. A bustle broke out somewhere, followed by loud laughter, Uncle Nicholas shouting: 'Girls, here are my presents,' and two little lambs ran into the ballroom. They wore red collars with Nina's name on one and mine on the other. We nearly swept Uncle Nicholas off his feet with our violent kisses. The boys had ponies—but those were left in the stables.

That golden evening went on. Presently I found a corner from where I could watch the lights on the tree, and I sat down in the floor, my Joan of Arc clasped in my arms. There, some time later, Cousin Sophie found me fast asleep.

# 7 *A great event at Trostnikovo*

The coming of the new year brought such wild weather that we were completely cut off from all the neighbours, and Cousin Sophie compared the drifts all along the drive and on the road with miniature Alps. Thick wet snow kept falling day in, day out. Whenever the wind freshened, snow drifted and formed really impassable mounds all over the place. Even our intrepid Kolia did not venture far beyond the stable-yard.

The two or three friends invited for Christmas had of sheer necessity to stay on. Otherwise we might have been in a beleaguered castle. We four kept very busy at our lessons once again and the Christmas holidays receded into the misty past. I led in history and German, but the others were far ahead of me in music, geography and particularly arithmetic. Figures always brought me to the edge of despair. Struggle as I would with the multiplication table, I usually ended by being defeated before I reached the middle. How I loathed the very sight of my little slate and the tiny sponge—as often as not soaked because of my tears! The stick of chalk always crumbled in my fingers.

One morning, when Cousin Sophie told me to multiply seven by seven, I started by scratching 7 plus 7 plus 7, and went no further. She looked over her shoulder and shook her head.

'Child, you are supposed to do multiplication, not addition.'

'What is the difference, Mamma?' I wailed, snatching at

that miserable little sponge. 'It won't come out—'

'Forty-nine, Katia,' whispered Kolia, but Cousin Sophie caught the whisper, and he was sent into a corner for fifteen minutes. Prompting was never forgiven at Trostnikovo.

Hard as we worked, in the evenings we had plenty of fun, with music, dancing, *tableaux-vivants* and games. One of the visitors, an alarmingly elegant gentleman from St. Petersburg, was devoted to ballet. He talked such a lot about Taglioni! Once Uncle Nicholas appeared, a white gauze scarf in his hands, and started pirouetting about in the middle of the hall. We four roared with laughter as we watched him trying to stand on his points. The elegant gentleman kept fiddling with his fob. At last he asked:

'May I ask what you are trying to do, Nicholas?'

'I am not Nicholas, my dear friend,' replied my cousins' father, his face perfectly grave, 'I am Taglioni.'

After that, the visitor did not indulge in further monologues in praise of the great dancer.

Nastia and Uncle Basil joined us in all the fun. One evening they danced *Rússkaya* together, he very handsome in a crimson silk shirt, white linen breeches and gleaming top boots, and Nastia in a pink *sárafan* falling down to the ankles, her white *kókosshnik* trimmed with silver braid. We watched them, entranced. When she dropped her handkerchief, Uncle Basil picked it up and we saw him press Nastia's fingers. Nina nudged my elbow and whispered:

'What did I tell you? He is devoted to her.'

But something far more important was about to happen at Trostnikovo.

We noticed that Aunt Marie hardly ever came into the schoolroom. Once at dinner we saw that she looked pale and barely touched her food. That very day, Kolia, watching by the window, saw Dr. Nikolaev come hurriedly across the courtyard.

'Is anyone ill?' we all wondered. Neither Cousin Sophie nor Nastia was with us, and Nina volunteered to find out.

She came back quickly enough, followed by old Nannie Lizbeth.

'Mamma?' cried the boys together, and their old nurse raised her hand.

'Now don't you get all flustered, my dears,' she said comfortably. 'Mamma is not at all ill, but she is going to have another baby, and the master thought the doctor should see her today—she is just off colour a bit. That is all.'

'When is the baby coming?'

'Soon enough,' replied Nannie Lizbeth rather cryptically, and Nina clapped her hands.

'Oh, how lovely—I do hope it will be a girl.'

'Certainly not,' retorted Kolia, 'there is Liza.'

Liza, the infant in arms whom I saw on my first day at Trostnikovo, was now a two-year-old bundle of energy, running all over the place and promising fair to follow in her brother's steps.

'And why shouldn't we have another sister?' demanded Volodia.

'Well, it is about time I had a real brother,' Kolia said so cuttingly that Volodia went scarlet and Nina shouted:

'How beastly, Kolia! Say you are sorry at once.'

'And why should I?' The boy clenched his little fists, and a quarrel would have flamed out then and there if old Lizbeth had not stopped it.

'Now then, dears, why waste time on shouting and fighting? Much better say a prayer or two for your mamma not to have too hard a time of it.'

We were in 1837. I cannot now remember when exactly Cousin Sophie told me about childbirth. Certainly, not one of us four had ever heard any stories about storks and gooseberry-bushes. We knew how a child came into the world and we knew it in a clean and direct manner. We were told, of course, that any baby was a gift of God. We were also told that its conception and birth was a holy and wonderful thing, something to be approached on tiptoe, as it were. We knew that the arrival of the baby would mean great suffering to Aunt Marie, and we also knew that the less we said about it, the better it would be for her—so old Lizbeth, who firmly believed in that ancient Russian superstition, had once told us.

Now Carnival drew nearer and nearer. One afternoon all of us together with Nastia were sent into the Blue Room. Mademoiselle Berg began reading aloud the story about a boy stolen by gypsies in infancy and brought up in a deep forest. The tale abounded in the most frightening and breathtaking adventures, and we listened eagerly enough, though we knew perfectly well the reason for us being all together in the Blue Room.

Our governess finished reading. The great house seemed strangely still. Kolia and Volodia busied themselves with a sketch. Nina and I began examining the exquisite embroidery Nastia was working at. Suddenly the door opened and old Lizbeth stood there, her eyes grave but her mouth smiling.

'Come,' she said, and went on: 'Be as quiet as you can, dears. Mamma is all right but very tired. It was not so bad, though, God be praised,' and she glanced almost mischievously at Kolia. 'You have got another brother— Anatole.'

She led us into a wing where a temporary bedroom had been arranged for Aunt Marie. We tiptoed in. In white, her lovely hair tumbled all over the pillows, she lay in bed, her face more radiant than I had ever seen it before. I remember that I wished I might go on looking at her for ever.

One by one, we went up to the bed, kissed her hand and congratulated her. She did not speak, but smiled at each one of us.

The infant, a white velvet coverlet trimmed with lace over him, lay on a wide sofa. Anatole's tiny wrinkled face did not seem at all attractive to me. I thought he was the ugliest baby I had seen, but my three cousins gasped in admiration, and I felt it was my duty to echo them.

By the time Carnival week came round the weather changed for the better and the roads were more or less passable. There was no question of any parties being held at Trostnikovo but all the grown-ups, including Nastia, went to several in the neighbourhood, and we were allowed to spend our evenings in Aunt Marie's bedroom. Sometimes we examined her jewels and her collection of antique intaglios. Sometimes she told us stories. Occasionally it amused us to plait and unplait her hair and arrange it into most fantastic coiffures. Once Kolia pulled at the plait so hard that poor Aunt Marie winced. Volodia shouted at his brother to stop. Kolia stopped and retorted:

'You mind your own business—'

'It is my business,' cried Volodia. 'You were hurting Mamma.'

'I was not—'

And in a minute the two were hard at it. Aunt Marie raised both hands.

'Must you two be always at loggerheads?' she asked.

'It was Kolia's fault, Mamma,' whimpered Volodia. 'Ask anyone! He is always up to some mischief. Everybody complains about him.'

'Nobody does—except you,' Kolia flung back. 'Silly little girl that you are! Cry-baby! Tell-tale!'

'Stop at once, Kolia,' Aunt Maria said severely. 'Volodia had the right to say what he did. He is your elder brother. You had no business to be rude. And you mustn't laugh at him so often either. I know how good you are at riding and games, but Volodia is far better at lessons and he does play the piano so well.'

'Why should I play the silly old piano?' Kolia muttered. 'A soldier need not tinker with music. I am going to be a hussar.'

'Well, darling, a lot of water will have flown under the bridge before your mother sees you in uniform,' said Aunt

67

Marie a little sadly.

Now we were in Lent. As usual, that put an end to dancing and the dolls' theatre. We were not taken to any services. None the less, Lent was kept at Trostnikovo in the strictly traditional manner in what concerned food. Uncle Nicholas would grumble at the absence of meat, cheese, butter and eggs, but Aunt Marie and Cousin Sophie argued that the annual change of diet was very good for one's health. I do not think that my adopted mother set any spiritual value on the Lenten regimen.

At that time Nastia took over our music lessons. She also offered to teach us to draw. She gave me up soon enough: I was incapable of tracing a single straight line without the help of a ruler! Aunt Marie wanted to teach me embroidery but Cousin Sophie thought it would be a waste of time.

'I would much rather Katia learned to knit. I would be pleased if she knitted even six pairs of stockings a year.'

The idea fired me at once. I imagined that the knitting-needles would immediately fly in my hands as fast as they did in Cousin Sophie's. Six pairs of stockings, indeed! I was certain I could do much more than that.

The very first knitting lesson brought bitter disillusionment. It took me ages to learn how to handle the needles: I either clutched them so hard that my fingers hurt, or held them so loosely that they all but slipped on the floor. Next, the counting of stitches seemed a nightmare.

'See how very simple it is, dearest,' said Cousin Sophie, having, as she hoped, started me on the right road at last. 'Four plain, four purl.'

'How many rows like that, Mamma?' I asked.

'Twenty-four, I think, for the stocking to fit really well.'

I thought in anguish:

'Twenty-four for each stocking... How many for two! Counting, counting all the time... Oh, goodness!'

Cousin Sophie left me, moved to her desk, and began

writing a letter. In less than a few minutes, I lost count of
the stitches, the wool got into a sorry tangle, and the
knitting-needles kept getting hotter and hotter. I puffed and
panted so loudly that Cousin Sophie laid down her pen.

'What in the world are you doing? Didn't I show you?'

And she took my hands in both hers, but I clenched my
sticky little fists so hard that one of the needles dug right
into her forefinger.

A trickle of blood spurted through the torn skin.

'Katia,' she exclaimed.

'I did not do it on purpose, Mamma,' I said dully. I so
hated the very sight of the wool and the knitting-needles
that it never even occurred to me to say I was sorry.

'Leave the room and do what you like,' she said dryly.

At the end of a passage I met Nastia who took me to the
ballroom to play a short piece, together with Volodia. Ten
minutes later Cousin Sophie came in and Nastia exclaimed:

'What in the world have you done to your hand, Sophie,
to get it bandaged?'

'Oh, I have hurt it by accident,' replied my adopted mother,
and I bent my burning face over the keys.

That afternoon I began feeling oddly seedy. My head ached.
There were strange noises in my ears and I could hardly
manage to eat my dinner. But Cousin Sophie's manner with
me was so pointedly distant that I did not like to say anything
to her.

In the night I must have had a frightening dream. I woke
up crying. Mademoiselle Berg at once ran in. In another
moment Cousin Sophie was bending over my bed, her cool
hand on my burning forehead.

'My darling, what is the matter?'

I mumbled something. She wrapped me up in a blanket
and carried me to her room.

That was the beginning of a vigil to last a fortnight. The
doctor diagnosed my illness as some kind of a fever due
to my too rapid growth. Night by night, my adopted mother

stayed in an armchair by my bed. She refused to let anyone else nurse me. Night by night, I lay, tossing on my little bed, most fantastic images crowding into my mind. I fell into an uneasy sleep and on waking saw her ready to attend to all my needs. Once she had said, 'You stand closest to me in the whole world.' That illness of mine proved her words. Clutching her cool hand in my sticky fingers, I knew myself safe and belonging to her wholly.

By day-time Cousin Sophie rested, and the children came to play with me when I began convalescing. Mademoiselle Berg, too, did her part. She and I began travelling all over the world together. Her stories were so vivid that I asked her:

'You must have been there and seen it all?'

'Oh no, child. I have found it all in books and learned much from my uncle who was a sailor.'

The discovery of the New World, the conquest of India, the life of trappers in Canada, the customs of negroes in Africa, the way of life in China, the coming of the Spaniards to South America, the history of tea, coffee, potatoes, tobacco, vines, spices and silkworms; in a word, everything that children of today find in numberless books, was told me by my governess by word of mouth and in a most compelling and interesting manner.

It proved a terribly slow convalescence. Easter was almost upon us when they permitted me to leave the bedroom, and I had rather a scare on Easter morning. The entire village came to the house after church to offer their congratulations to master and mistress, to exchange the traditional triple kiss with them, and to receive an egg painted red. When I heard some of the peasants say to the butler that they would like to receive the triple kiss from the young ladies and gentlemen, I ran and hid myself in a corner of one of the drawing-rooms. The mere idea of kissing such a multitude of men, women and children made me shake with fear.

# 8 *Getting ready for a long journey*

That spring, Aunt Marie's mother, whom I had not yet met and whom everybody called 'Grand-maman', invited the whole family to come down south to her at Matzovka, a big place near Poltava. Grand-maman must have heard that her daughter's health, having never been robust, was weakened after Anatole's arrival. Grand-maman thought that, after a few months at Matzovka, Aunt Marie should go abroad for a cure, accompanied by her second sister, Lena.

It was true that everybody felt anxious about Aunt Marie. She complained of nothing, but she often looked tired and pale and she developed a cough. Again, little Anatole was almost always ailing, and even a famous doctor from Kiev could not do much for him.

Grand-maman's plans, however, did not please Uncle Nicholas at all.

'I have no use for all those famous German spas,' he said. 'Next year Marie and I will make for the Caucasus—its air and waters are far better. As to Matzovka, we might go down there—but not before August. I want to rebuild parts of the house and the architect writes he can't start before the autumn.'

So we settled down for the summer at Trostnikovo.

I must confess that the two lambs given to Nina and me at Christmas soon lost their attraction for us—chiefly because they grew and grew, and by June they were sent off to join the flock. That summer our greatest pleasure out of doors was our very first kitchen-garden. Uncle Nicholas ordered that a sizeable plot just off the orchards was to be allotted to us; the head gardener gave us seeds, together with many instructions, and Aunt Marie presented us with a set of garden tools bought at Kursk. Nina and I were told that the kitchen-garden was to be our sole responsibility. We learned digging, planting, hoeing, trenching and weeding, and we were thrilled to see the first seedlings shooting up from our tidy beds. It was indeed a proud occasion when we brought two bunches of radishes to the table. Presently we had lettuce, and last of all peas and carrots. Nina and I had hoped that we would be able to cook those vegetables ourselves, but Aunt Marie looked doubtful, and Cousin Sophie refused to allow it.

'I shall soon start teaching you plain cooking, but to have you messing with your vegetables in the kitchen, is out of the question. You would be in everyone's way.'

Our stay at Matzovka was to last till the following May. Already in early July the hall and the breakfast-room began getting crowded with huge wooden trunks barred with broad strips of iron. There were eight of us in the family, not counting little Anatole, and about a dozen servants were to accompany us, and that meant taking mountains of luggage.

At first, the prospect of the journey did not attract me at all. Nina and Volodia kept assuring me that I would fall in love with Matzovka at first sight because of its marvellous winter-garden and its orchards where almonds, walnuts and grapes grew in the open air. Nina sang eloquent praises of Nadia, Aunt Marie's youngest sister, who was many years younger than Grand-maman's other children. Nadia, said Nina, was such fun, and everything would be just glorious at Matzovka. I listened to it all and kept repeating that I had no wish to leave Trostnikovo, and Kolia, who had never been to Matzovka, upheld me every time.

But, little by little, I grew accustomed to the coming change. Cousin Sophie, preoccupied as she was with countless household arrangements, had far less leisure for us. Our lessons, of course, were not interrupted, but we had much greater freedom during the rest of the day.

Preparations for our departure grew more and more exciting every day, and Kolia and I would rush from room to room, watching the servants at their work as though nothing could have got done without us two being present. Kolia's close companionship had already turned me into a tomboy. He had taught me—all in secret—to climb trees and to leap over gates, and even indoors I often raced along as though a wild beast were at my heels. Poor Mademoiselle Berg was in despair and Cousin Sophie kept scolding me. I tried to preserve a ladylike demeanour when either of them happened to be about, but, whenever left to myself, I followed in Kolia's footsteps most faithfully—even to the extent of sliding down the banisters one afternoon.

One Sunday morning Cousin Sophie had a new and rather elaborate pinafore for me to try on. It had prettily edged pockets and lacing back and front. She found something wrong with the left shoulder, marked the place with pins, and told me to go to the breakfast-room where the dress-maker was awaiting the verdict. We were in one of the smaller drawing-rooms. My way led through the Green Room, down a short passage ending at the door to the breakfast-room. At once I rushed off as though the house were on fire.

'Gently, gently, Katia,' Cousin Sophie called out after me. 'Don't you go and tumble at the corner.'

The echoes of her voice still rang in my ears when my foot caught at the threshold of the breakfast-room, and I fell, hitting my head hard against an enormous trunk standing close to the door. With a shriek—'Please don't tell Mamma'—I lost consciousness.

I came round in Aunt Marie's arms. I was dimly aware of blood running down my face and neck. People were bustling about. I vaguely saw Dr. Nikolaev bending over me, something thing, long and shining in his hands. In an instant he began putting stitches into my forehead. I cannot remember being conscious of any pain during the operation. I closed my eyes and heard someone crying somewhere. Much later Nina would tell me that it was poor Cousin Sophie, a fool of a footman having run to her to announce that the fall had killed me.

They did not keep me in bed for very long, but I felt most humiliatingly groggy on getting up. They cut my hair off and shaved it round the wound. I was told I would have to wear a bandage for at least six weeks. And nobody, beginning with Cousin Sophie, ever reproached me for an accident due to my own thoughtlessness. I had learned my lesson the hard way, and that seemed enough.

About a month later, I think, we left Trostnikovo. Our train consisted of six vehicles, one of them drawn by eight horses. Cousin Sophie, Mademoiselle Berg, the two boys and I, together with Fat Dasha holding little Liza in her arms, travelled in an enormous but exceptionally well-sprung dormeuse.

To reach Matzovka we had to travel nearly five hundred miles, and we travelled at the hottest time of the year. I cannot remember how many days it took us to get to Grandmaman's place. We did not hurry. There were so many regular daily stops for meals—always in the open air, the food cooked by the men we had with us. We never travelled by night, but I have no recollections of any inns except the very last one. My head ached, my appetite had gone, and I slept badly. Cousin Sophie's usual severity now was as though it had never been. All my wishes were answered. She even kept fruit and milk in the dormeuse in case I got hungry on the road.

The farther south we went, the sharper grew the changes in the landscape. We were in the very heart of the Ukraine, the whitewashed huts of its hamlets standing in huge orchards, every tree laden with ripening fruit. Oxen instead of horses drew the peasant carts. The embroidered clothes of the women gleamed in the sun. What rivers we passed ran like silver, and we could not follow the people's speech—at once so like and unlike Russian.

One afternoon a terrific storm broke over our heads. When it eased off, the air got most gratefully cooler, and we leant our heads out of the dormeuse windows. Suddenly our train came to a halt, and in an instant there was Uncle Nicholas. Kolia shouted:

'How much longer now, Papa?'

'We are close to the last posting inn,' he replied. 'Sophie, I wanted to know if Katia is all right. It was such a storm, wasn't it?'

'Her head is none too good,' replied my adopted mother. 'I shall be truly thankful to get to Matzovka, Nicholas.'

'Tomorrow afternoon,' he told her and went back to his own carriage in front.

In half an hour our train lumbered its way to the posting inn well known to my cousins. I saw an ugly wooden one-storied building with a great garden rioting at the back. Whilst the servants were carrying in the things we needed for the night, an enormously fat woman in a bright blue gown and a green apron came out to greet us. Aunt Marie and Uncle Nicholas hailed her as an old friend.

'Well, Stepanida, all going well?'

'Yes, sir,' she answered in a thick, comfortable voice, 'except that the pigs sickened at Easter.'

Our coachman came to carry me out of the dormeuse. The fat woman stared at my bandaged head, sighed, and asked Uncle Nicholas:

'And who might the little lady be, sir? Quite unlike all the other children.'

'She is our cousin,' he told her, 'daughter of Madame Berquovist.'

It was dim and cool in the main room of the inn. We had supper. Uncle Nicholas and the boys were going to spend the night in the open air. For the rest of us, lots of fragrant hay were brought into the room, and the maids contrived to make very comfortable beds with blankets and sheets.

For the first time since leaving Trostnikovo, I slept soundly and woke late, the morning sun gilding the room. There was nobody there but Nina. All the hay and the bedding had been cleared away except for my corner.

'Katia.' Nina ran up to me. 'Get up, darling—it is such a marvellous morning. We are going to feed in the garden. Everybody is gone down to the river. I was told to guard you here.'

'Are we leaving soon?' I asked, and began putting on my shoes and stockings.

'No, Papa wants the horses to have a good rest. But it is only thirty miles to Grand-maman's. We'll be there in the afternoon.'

The small windows were wide open. The fragrance of coffee and new bread made me feel hungry for the first time since my illness. I hurried with my dressing, and Nina and I ran into the garden. By the little gate we met old Stepanida. Her small eyes peered at me with curiosity, and she asked Nina the same question she had put to Uncle Nicholas the day before. I disliked her intensely.

Nina explained in far greater detail.

'Katia is Cousin Sophie's adopted daughter. Her own mother is dead.'

'Ah,' said Stepanida, 'now I understand. . . . Poor little orphan,' and she patted me on the cheek with her glossy fat hand. The unwanted caress so infuriated me that I sprinted away towards a little rose arbour at the end of a lawn bordered by very tall limes. A big table, already laid for the meal, stood there.

Nina raced after me and we sat down on the bench in the arbour.

'I hate such fat old women,' I said angrily, 'and how dare she call me an orphan?'

'She did not mean any harm, Katia. And you *are* an orphan. You have no mamma—'

'What do you mean?' I stared at Nina. 'Cousin Sophie is

my mamma.'

'Not really,' Nina stammered. 'I mean her surname is not the same as yours, is it?'

'What does that matter?' I said fiercely. 'From the very beginning she said she was my mamma.'

Nina looked at me rather oddly. Suddenly I felt she had something on her mind. I dared not ask.

She bit her lip.

'Katia, I am afraid you don't know'—she began very timidly.

'What?' I sat up, and my heart took to beating faster and faster.

'No, no, I must not tell you.'

'You have got to tell me,' I cried. 'I shan't give you a moment's peace till you tell me.'

'Well,' she still hesitated, 'promise on your honour not to give me away.'

'I do.'

'Well, Katia, there is a big secret—oh dear, I really don't know how to tell you.'

'Nina, darling,' I begged her, 'you must—'

'And you won't cry?'

'Is it something to cry about?'

'Well, I don't know . . . Darling, your papa is going to marry again.'

'What?' I gasped.

'Yes. He wants you to have a mamma—someone like my own—you know—to live in the same house with him and to bear his name. The wedding will be quite soon.'

'Nina,' I said very slowly, 'how is it that you know all about it?'

'Well, it was soon after your illness. Your papa sent a letter to Cousin Sophie and she showed it to Mamma. I was there—but they did not make me promise not to tell. It seems that everybody is angry with him because of your own mamma. Cousin Sophie cried her eyes out that morning. She said she had never expected it of him. She did love your mamma awfully much, didn't she?'

'Yes,' I replied, and two tears rolled down my cheeks. Nina got scared.

'Katia, angel, darling, you mustn't cry. Cousin Sophie will tell you all about it. You were so poorly at home she did not want to upset you.'

'Did you hear if Papa wants me back?' I asked and began fumbling for my little handkerchief.

'Something was said about you in the letter, but I did not quite understand it. I do remember that Cousin Sophie kept repeating, "I shan't give her up. She belongs to me. No step-mother shall see her." Yes,' Nina nodded her curly head, 'I do remember that.'

A great burden fell off my shoulders at those words and I dried my eyes quickly. But my thoughts were in a maze. Cousin Sophie and the Trostnikovo family were now my life. I never spoke of my father and brothers to anyone, and hardly ever thought of them. Nobody at Tver had written to me since I left, or remembered my existence at Christmas or my birthday. That part of my tiny chronicle was finished for good, as I thought, and I could not even recall my father's face. Yet even the remote possibility that I might have to part from Cousin Sophie filled me with burning impatience to see her come back from the river. When I saw her at last, I ran into her arms. 'Mamma, Mamma, my dearest, dearest Mamma,' I kept muttering, and she answered my caresses with her own.

Presently we were on the road. Everybody was asleep in the dormeuse except Cousin Sophie and myself, and we began talking about Matzovka.

'What is Nadia like, Mamma?' I wanted to know.

Cousin Sophie paused before replying.

'She is very bright and intelligent, but rather spoilt, I fear. And she can be most provoking at times. But do try to make friends with her, Katia. Grand-maman and Lena are angelic.

But now I must tell you that our routine at Matzovka is certain to be somewhat disrupted. The boys are growing up. They will shortly be going to a boarding-school in Kiev, and Uncle Nicholas wishes them to be coached by a Swiss tutor at a neighbour's place. I am sure that Nina will spend quite a lot of time with Nadia. So there will be just you, my little daughter, in the classroom.'

'I see,' I said slowly. 'Oh, Mamma, I do wish we had not left Trostnikovo. I would like to spend all my life there.'

Cousin Sophie laughed.

'That is out of all question. My own plans are quite different. I think we won't be there very much longer, Katia—'

Here the story told by Nina flashed through my mind. I blushed vehemently and turned my face to the window.

'By the way, child,' she went on in a studiedly indifferent voice, 'you are going to have a stepmother soon.'

I bit my lips and turned my face with an effort—but I managed to keep my promise to the end. The words 'Yes, I know' were not spoken.

'Your father is getting married to a very pretty girl,' went on my adopted mother, 'the daughter of a local landowner.'

'I shan't love her.' I spoke through clenched teeth.

She laughed.

'But you won't have anything to do with her, dearest. On our way north—in a few years' time—we shall stop at Tver to see your father, and then we will go on to Italy and settle down somewhere near the sea.'

'I shall never call her "Mamma",' I went on vehemently.

'I am your mamma. You were left to me by your own dear mother, and I am determined to keep the promise given to her—to live solely for you. And what is more, your father will probably have other children and I should say he is quite pleased not to have you with him.'

I flung my arms round her neck.

'Don't send me back there, Mamma,' I mumbled. 'I love

you so.'

'Send you back, child? Don't worry your poor head with such a foolish idea. You are my little daughter,' and she kissed me tenderly.

That very instant my headache vanished. I felt well. I was gay. I chattered all the way to the gates of Matzovka.

## 9 *Another world to learn . . .*

Certainly, it was another world for me to learn. The sight of the slow-moving oxen along the roads of Poltava Province proved to be but a preface. It was good that we still had Fat Dasha and Olga to look after us—the Ukrainian spoken by the maids was not always easy to understand. The daily pace was more leisurely, and in the early afternoon even stable-boys slept in the sun. Within the great one-storied house the day's routine beat to a different rhythm, and its echoes could not be excluded even from the wing appointed to us.

The glories of Matzovka had not been exaggerated by my little cousins. The enormous winter-garden lying at the back of a big dim drawing-room took my breath away: I had not seen such trees and plants except on pictures and engravings. I could not believe that such rich colours existed in nature. The winding paths, carpeted with yellow sand, were fringed by myrtles, banana-trees, palms, lemon, orange and mulberry trees. Green and crimson parrots had a big gilt cage at the end of a path, but it stood wide open, and the parrots rather scared me at first. Unfamiliar and lovely trees were also in the park, which boasted a lake with a small island in the middle. It was all new and exciting, and I felt grateful to Cousin Sophie for the fortnight's holiday she gave us.

There were Grand-maman and her second daughter, Lena, much younger than Aunt Marie, and my adopted mother had been right about those two. They were truly angelic. Grand-maman, whose slightly faded beauty reminded me of Aunt Marie's, kissed me warmly on arrival and said:

'Remember that here you are just as much at home as at Trostnikovo.'

Pretty Lena's brown eyes smiled into mine.

'Sophie, how big Katia is! I had imagined that she was quite little.'

And there was Nadia, only three years older than myself, thin and wiry, her black eyes full of mischief, her manner most provocative. She tore into the room like a bombshell, upsetting a small table on the way. She stared at me hard, something like a contemptuous smile on her lips.

'This is little Katia, Nadia,' said Grand-maman, 'and I want you two to be great friends.'

'Oh,' said Nadia. She brushed my cheek with her lips, and ran away, shouting to Nina to follow her. Later, at tea, I sat and marvelled all to myself. Nadia behaved like a spoilt child of five. She would pick up a cake, take a bite, throw it away, take another, smell it, and push it towards her neighbour. Then she would jump off her chair, run to her eldest sister and Uncle Nicholas, kiss and hug them, come back to her own place and chatter at the top of her voice. I saw Nina's eyes follow her admiringly and I marvelled more and more because Grand-maman said nothing to put a stop to all the pranks which would have been quite impossible at Trostnikovo.

I remember that after tea I looked for Nina and could not find her. The grown-ups were all talking in the drawing-room, and I did not dare to follow them there. I was lost until a footman showed me the way to our wing. I sat by a window in an unfamiliar schoolroom. Nothing except the thought of Cousin Sophie being in the house brought me any comfort.

Not until bedtime did I see Nina again. She ran in, gay, excited.

'Where have you been?' I asked a little sulkily.

'Oh, with Nadia! You see, she and I have not seen each other for such ages... We had heaps and heaps to tell each other, Katia. And do you know—' and she started chattering about Grand-maman's rooms, about Lena's collection of tiny porcelain dolls, about Nadia's beautiful French desk, her clothes, her garnet necklace, her books. Nina would have gone on for ages if Cousin Sophie had not come in and told us to say our prayers and get into bed.

I did not sleep very well that night. I felt so utterly lost. I remembered a warning once given me by Kolia: 'Nina is all right but she is a bit of a weathercock. If Lili had stayed for a fortnight, you would not have seen much of Nina—she would have stuck to Lili all the day long.' I had not then believed him. I loved Nina so much, she was the first friend I ever had, and we had become like sisters to each other. And I kept asking myself whether it was not just the first day's impressions that had upset me.

Alas, as days grew into weeks, Nina moved further and further away from me.

Our life was altogether changed. Every day Volodia and Kolia were driven away to some neighbour's house to have their lessons with a Swiss tutor. When the weather worsened, they sometimes spent the night there. Cousin Sophie continued to teach Nina but not every day. My little friend often spent hours and hours in that part of the house where I felt I might not go without being invited. I knew she accompanied Nadia to a great-uncle's in the neighbourhood and to other houses and that, together with Nadia, she sat in the drawing-room whenever guests came to Matzovka. In a word, Nina's life began flowing to a pattern in which I had no share. True that every evening she would tell me all about her day, but that was not enough. I felt excluded, pushed out into the cold. I did not like speaking of such things to Cousin Sophie. Grand-maman and Lena, for all their sweetness to me, were still strangers. Nastia was not at Matzovka. I loved Nina far too much to quarrel with her. So I took to brooding and ended by hating Nadia.

Soon enough I saw that the feeling was mutual. Quite unwittingly Grand-maman added fuel to the fire by frequently saying to her youngest daughter:

'Oh Nadia, dearest, could you not follow Katia's example? She is nearly three years younger than you and how much more she knows! Really, darling, you must not be so lazy.'

Nadia would kiss her mother, shrug and run away. She did not dare to attack me if Grand-maman, Aunt Marie or Lena were there, but she had plenty of opportunities at other times. During luncheon, served to us at a different time from the meal of the grown-ups, once her chair happened to be placed next to mine, she would push it away.

'A silly fool like myself should not sit next to a prodigy,' she would mock in such a way that it was I who became a silly little fool. I tried hard to ignore it all but I knew that my mouth was trembling.

Mademoiselle Berg understood neither French nor Russian. The boys were not there, and Nina laughed. She thought Nadia was joking. But I knew those were not jokes. Malice was an art Nadia had learned to perfection. The day she caught me out in a slip in French, she had a large bowl placed in front of my plate.

'For your tears,' she explained. 'A prodigy, as they all say you are, must be so unhappy at having made a mistake. Now you can cry as much as you like.'

When a dish of sausages was served at luncheon, she shouted to the butler:

'Alexander, Alexander, mind you put a lot on her plate. Everybody says the Germans live on sausages.'

One Sunday morning the boys were there, and I had a very happy time racing to the lake with Kolia. Then he ran off to the stables, and Nadia saw me come back to the balcony, my hair dishevelled, a flounce torn off my dress, and a stocking right down to the ankle, a garter having been shed during the run.

Nina, unfortunately, was not with us. Nobody but

Nadia and Volodia sat on the balcony steps. She sneered at me:

'They should dress you in a boy's clothes! What a sight you are!'

Volodia said quietly:

'Well, Katia is on her way to get tidy. What does it matter?'

'Oh, nothing, I suppose—' Nadia jerked her shoulders impatiently—'except that she always gets into trouble, doesn't she? Anyone would have thought that banging her head against a trunk would have taught her a lesson! No wonder she is never taken to parties! Why, she would disgrace us all by climbing a tree or something! A tomboy—'

This was a bit too much. I burst out:

'All right! Let me be a tomboy and a disgrace to you all. And you are just beastly and unkind. I can't bear you!'

'Do you think I can bear you?' she retorted. 'Mamma told me to treat you like a sister! Rubbish! I loathe you! You don't belong to us! You are a foreigner, a miserable little orphan. I suppose Cousin Sophie took you out of charity.'

I burst into tears. For the first time I saw Volodia lose his temper. His colour heightened, he clenched his fists.

'Nadia, how dare you?' he shouted. 'Do you want me to go and tell Grand-maman? How dare you say such awful things? They are all untrue—Katia is our sister.'

Volodia's championship scared Nadia more than my tears. She mumbled an awkward apology and ran away.

'Katia, darling,' Volodia said to me, 'take no notice of her.'

'I hate Matzovka,' I sobbed. 'I wish we were going home.'

'We are not going to stay here for ever,' he comforted me.

Volodia's spirited words did not lose their virtue for a few days. Nadia either ignored me or spoke civilly enough. Yet soon after the arrival of her English governess, Miss Cottle, Nadia and I crossed swords again. To tell the truth, it was partly my own fault.

Nadia had her English lessons in Lena's sitting-room. Within a few weeks, happening to be there all by myself, I suddenly felt very curious about Nadia's progress in English. I opened a notebook and bent over the table, leafing one ink-stained page after another. The door was flung open and Nadia rushed in.

'What are you meddling with my things for?' she shouted.

I answered in a level voice:

'Just looking at your English exercises! They are full of mistakes. I am sorry for Miss Cottle.'

'And what has that to do with you?'

'Nothing at all—but you are older than I am and how shockingly you write!'

'Not worse than you.' Nadia stamped her foot. 'I have seen your squiggles.'

'I am much younger. There will be time for me to learn properly.'

Nadia flung the notebook into a drawer, locked it, dropped the key into her pocket, and laughed unpleasantly.

'Of course, you must work hard at your studies since you are going to be a governess.'

'Who is going to be a governess?' Lena's indignant voice rang from the doorway, and Nadia answered cuttingly:

'Your little pet!'

'You mean Katia? And why should you think she is going to be a governess?'

'What is to happen to her once Cousin Sophie is dead?'

Never had I seen Lena so angry.

'Nadia, you have a nasty tongue and a wicked heart. Mamma has spoilt you too much. Ask Katia's pardon at once, do you hear?'

'Why should I? I found her rummaging in my papers. I have not done anything.'

'Yes, you have! To stand there insulting a guest in your own house! Cheap and mean! Put yourself in her place! Would you like to be treated so rudely?'

Nadia said nothing. Nor did she move.

'Well? Do you want me to tell Mamma? Volodia told me something a few days ago. Would you like Mamma to hear all about it?'

Nadia started uneasily. The idea that the mother whom she adored might learn of her tricks and unkindnesses seemed to make her hesitate. Reluctantly enough she came up to me, brushed her lips against my cheek and mumbled:

'Forgive me. My fault...'

At that moment my hatred of Nadia seemed to melt away. Without knowing why, I felt desperately sorry for her. I pulled her towards me and answered her kiss with a warm one of my own, and the truce between us continued for quite a time. When my birthday came, Nadia even had a present for me—a beautiful folding panorama with the views of Wiesbaden. As we all stood admiring it, Lena said:

'I hope, Katia, you will like it as much as I did. You will see it one day, you know. In two or three years Cousin Sophie will take you abroad.'

'And what about Volodia and me?' asked Kolia.

'Ah, no, you are going to a school at Kiev.'

We all looked at one another. Lena's words did no more than confirm many hints we had heard since arriving at Matzovka. Apparently, our days at Trostnikovo were not going on indefinitely. I loved that place with all my heart and I loved Nina—but in all truth I felt that I could be happy anywhere so long as I had my adopted mother with me. So I thought at the time. Later my feeling came to be qualified: anywhere except at Matzovka...

One November evening we were all gathered together in Grand-maman's sitting-room. At breakfast that day Cousin Sophie had said that I would be expected to read aloud to the grown-ups before supper. The book chosen by her was *Thérèse ou la petite soeur de charité*, a story extremely popular among older children of that time. I felt terribly nervous when I began, but presently I got so immersed in the story that I forgot everything else, and I had come to a most interesting place when Cousin Sophie put down her needle-work and told me to stop till next time.

'Dear Katia, how well you read aloud,' said Grand-maman, 'so does my Nadia—but she never seems to find any time.'

'Let her read something now,' suggested Cousin Sophie, who was very pleased with my tiny success but also anxious not to let such unaccustomed praise feed my vanity.

The evening went on very pleasantly with poetry and sing-ing. A chorus finished, I exclaimed:

'I wish our Nastia were here!'

'She will be here very soon—in early December,' smiled Aunt Marie.

'And what a Christmas we are going to have!' cried Nina. 'With Uncle Basil, too! Charades and dancing—'

'And fortune-telling!' Nadia joined in.

Cousin Sophie shook her head.

'Yes, in a word fun and more fun—just for our own selves! And we might remember that this poor village has had many disasters since last Christmas—appalling fires and cattle sickness, too. I am afraid the peasants' children are not likely to have much fun—and I am just wondering whether we might not give them a real Christmas—a tree and lots of presents.' She paused.

'Presents, Cousin Sophie?' echoed Nadia. 'You mean toys and sweets?'

'Certainly not only those,' Nina broke in to my great pleasure. 'Cousin Sophie means warm clothes and caps and suchlike—and everything to be made by ourselves.'

'Yes, Nina,' my adopted mother nodded, and I felt in-tensely proud of her.

'By ourselves?' drawled Nadia. 'There are crowds of children—and just eight weeks left till Christmas. We'll never get ready—'

And wasn't I most wickedly pleased that nobody took much notice of Nadia's objections? Uncle Nicholas at once plunged his hand into a pocket and flung a few gold coins on the table. 'If that is not enough for all your flannel and stuff, let me know,' he said. Grand-maman thought that her grey woollen dressing-gown might cut up for boys' jackets, and Aunt Marie offered her dark blue merino for girls' kirtles. Mademoiselle Berg volunteered to knit babies' caps and blankets. Little by little, even Nadia was fired by the idea, and that very evening we elected Lena to be our cutter-in-chief.

'What can we do?' asked Volodia.

'You and Kolia,' Lena replied, 'can make little boxes for sweets, and gild walnuts. We shall want lots of those for the tree.'

Within the next two days a big room in our wing became a veritable workshop. Two long tables were covered by masses of flannel, calico, cotton of all colours, and knitting wool. Bad weather kept us indoors and we spent all our leisure hours getting ready for what we called 'our own Christmas'. I did not shine as a needlewoman, nor could I knit, but I persevered with my hemming. True that my first efforts provoked many a barbed remark of Nadia's, but we were far too busy to quarrel.

At the end of November we welcomed our dear Nastia. With her usual vivacity she at once flung herself into all our plans.

'And, my dears, I have an idea of my own—let us have a surprise for the grown-ups. Lena says that Grand-maman is planning to give us a grand tea after the party. That will be the moment to give our presents to them.'

Sewing momentarily forgotten, we hung on Nastia's words.

'Let us begin with Aunt Marie,' said Nastia, and Nina cried:

'I'll give Mamma the Dresden coffee-cup that Grandpapa

gave me. She likes it so much.'

After the boys and Nadia had made their own suggestions, I hesitated and at last decided to embroider a bookmark. Grand-maman was to have a footstool from us all, Uncle Nicholas our silhouettes, Cousin Sophie some handkerchiefs marked by us and put into a box, to be made by Volodia and Kolia.

'Gracious!' exclaimed Nadia. 'Your idea is wonderful, Nastia, but we'll never be ready with all that work for the village on top of it. We had better get four or five girls from the sewing-room to help us.'

'Certainly not,' said Nina, pouting. 'That would spoil everything.'

Well, all the gifts for the peasant children and our surprises for the grown-ups were certainly ready by Christmas Eve. After a hurried breakfast we ran into the ballroom to parcel up all the clothes, blankets, babies' shoes and caps we had made. Each parcel was neatly labelled with a name from a list prepared for us by Uncle Nicholas. The substantial presents piled on two enormously long trestles, we began decorating the tree. Such masses of things had been given to us—lovely little lanterns shaped like apples and pears, coloured glass balls, chocolate dolls and animals, gingerbread, pink sugar mice, and all sorts of other things. The tree decorated from top to bottom, quite a lot of the stuff remained, and we began wrapping it all up in red and blue paper and adding those packages to the more substantial presents. Lena was the only grown-up to help us. Not even Mademoiselle Berg came into the ballroom. From time to time Cousin Sophie would look in, make no comment and go away. We all felt the day belonged to us wholly and we were determined to do everything as well as we could.

Candles were lit about four o'clock in the afternoon, and we four, supported by Nadia, Nastia and Lena, took our stand behind the trestles. When the doors were flung open, I gasped. I had no idea there could have been such a crowd of children in just one village, and all of them came with their mothers and grandmothers.

For the first few moments it almost looked as though our wonderful party would never come off. The children huddled by the doors, staring at the tree. Quite a number began whimpering. A few howled loudly, and none would come forward even after Lena had called out some of the names. Then a red-cheeked little girl, wrapped in very shabby sheepskins, came forward shyly, thumb to her mouth, her eyes riveted on the tree. Lena at once handed her the two parcels, and her yell of pleasure reassured the others that there were no wild bears lurking in the corners of the ballroom.

For something like three hours or longer, we four, pink with excitement, stood and handed over the presents. I remember that the very last little guest, far bolder than the others, decided to unwrap her smaller package then and there. Gingerbread, some gilded walnuts and sugar mice fell on the floor—so absorbed was she in a chocolate lady with red ribbon at her throat. She held it up, she stared at it, her brown eyes enormous. Then she shouted to her mother, '*Mamka, mamka*, I have got a baby,' and hugged the chocolate lady so hard that the head snapped in two. I felt so sorry because there was nothing else I could offer. Suddenly Nadia dived into a box under the trestle and produced a slightly dusty but otherwise undamaged chocolate cat. I was so happy to give it to the child and felt like hugging Nadia, but she made a face at me and ran away.

Weary but happy, we ran to Lena's sitting-room. Grandmaman had ordered a superb tea-supper by way of rewarding us, and how pleased were the grown-ups with our 'surprises'. We enjoyed all the good things on the table, talked and laughed almost till midnight, the very first time we four were allowed to sit up.

But the excitement of Christmas soon came to an end, and my unshared misery continued deepening. Hardly a day passed but Nadia contrived an opportunity to hurt me where it hurt most. She was clever enough never to do it in anyone's presence, and I dared not complain. Such bottling-up ended by affecting my work and my temper. Arithmetic became a nightmare once again. Cheeses and their weights maddened me. I just could not understand why one cheese should weigh a pound and a half if four cheeses of the same size weighed six pounds. Practically every lesson began and ended in misery.

'Katia, what in the name of goodness is happening to you?' asked Cousin Sophie, one particularly dreadful morning when, having first thrown my little slate on the floor, I crumbled the chalk all over the desk. 'I had to leave you without dessert three times last week. You are wearing me out with your tantrums. Always tears and screams! Really, if you go on like that much longer, I might lose my patience and have you sent back to your father.'

But even that terrible threat made no impression on me.

'Well, do so,' I shouted. 'I hate arithmetic, I hate Matzovka, I hate everybody. Yes, I hate everybody,' I repeated, my whole body shaking with fury.

Just at that moment Aunt Marie, her face very pale, opened the door.

'Sophie, what is the matter with Katia?'

'I can't tell you, Marie. It has been going on for nearly a month now. Tears, tears and temper! Look what she has done with her slate. It may well be that the air of Matzovka does not agree with her... I can't tell.'

Meanwhile, I lay huddled in a corner of the sofa, my burning, swollen face turned to the wall. Aunt Marie sat down by me and began stroking my head. I did not stir.

'Leave her alone, Marie. She has just told me that she does not love any of us any more.'

'Why?' And Aunt Marie began tickling my neck. 'You naughty, naughty kitten, what have we done to you?'

'Nothing,' I mumbled.

'Now turn round,' she went on gently. 'Sit up and tell Mamma and me what it is all about.'

'I hate arithmetic,' I muttered, and turned, but kept my head bent.

'Well, darling, does arithmetic mater so much? Must you always upset poor Mamma and ruin your health because of it? Why, It came out of my room to find out if there had been some terrible accident in the schoolroom—you were screaming so. Do you think Mamma can go on putting up with it? Listen, kitten, you must begin taking care of her. To think that nasty arithmetic should have turned our good, dear Katia into a wild tiger-cub! I just don't believe it. And do you think it would be easy for Mamma to part with you?'

I gulped hard and raised my head. There sat Cousin Sophie, such a sad smile on her face that I rushed to her.

'Mamma, Mamma, please don't send me away. I am sorry. I promise to do better.'

And it so happened that I kept the promise to the very end. Never again was Cousin Sophie subjected to a scene in the classroom. I made no great progress with those hateful sums, but, at least, I would not let them drive me to fury.

The coming of an exquisite spring was heartening. I knew we would soon be returning to Trostnikovo, and little by little Nadia's taunts ceased to provoke my anger.

Of course, it was she who poisoned my stay at Matzovka. I was too small to understand it at the time and felt still further confused by the fact that Nadia's moods were as unpredictable as the weather in England. For days on end she would mock, tease and hurt me. Then for no rhyme or reason she would seek me out, shower kisses on me, even give me presents, and assure me that she loved me dearly. I could not make her out at all.

## 10 *First sorrow*

It was not Nina but her brothers who shared my feelings about Matzovka. As our stay there drew to an end, they began complaining to me of the strictness of their tutor. There was more: they had not the freedom of the stables, and Kolia in particular complained that every time he wanted a ride, elaborate arrangements had to be made with a neighbour's head-groom since there were no suitable mounts for him at Matzovka. Lena did not ride, and Grand-maman would not have known a moment's peace if Nadia had taken to the saddle. Volodia grumbled that Matzovka had neither the space nor the light of Trostnikovo. Matzovka's rooms were large enough but rather cluttered with furniture, the ceilings were low, and the windows over-curtained.

'And oh dear, what ages they always sit at table,' moaned Kolia.

All these grievances were shared with me in secret, and I am rather ashamed to admit that I began feeling much happier.

At last the date was fixed for the departure, the spring floods having receded rather early that year. Kolia and I were hard put to it not to look happy when we were saying good-bye to Grand-maman and her daughters. I cannot tell about Kolia but I certainly had not succeeded, because the very moment after our dormeuse had driven through the big gates, Cousin Sophie said:

'Katia, dearest, Grand-maman and Lena have been so kind to you, and you looked as though you were in a hurry to get into the carriage.'

'Well, Mamma,' I answered carefully, 'it is always good to get back home.'

Cousin Sophie shook her head, and I had a feeling that she knew much more about my wars with Nadia than I had imagined.

I also knew that Grand-maman and Nadia would be coming to Trostnikovo the following year. Strangely enough, the prospect did not trouble me in the least.

All four of us went nearly mad with joy as soon as we saw the stone wall of the park. There were no lessons for nearly a week, the magnificent weather held, and we raced through the gardens, the orchards and the park, anxious to see each beloved corner again. The orchards were so many clouds of delicate pink and white, the flower-beds in front of the house blazed with glory, and not one of us regretted the exotic setting of the famous winter-garden of Matzovka. We were at home. It was paradise.

Except for just one thing. It was not very obvious when we four happened to be all together, but once Nina and I happened to be by our own two selves, we each felt there was something of a gulf between us, and quite a few days had gone by before Nina started explaining.

'Katia, darling, don't hold it against me that I spent so much time with Nadia. Grand-maman would arrange things for us to do together, and what could I do?'

'Oh,' I said rather dully and stared at a lime in full blossom. 'Indeed?' I said after a pause and tried to look as indifferent as I could, but my mouth shook a little.

'I could not always help it,' stammered Nina, 'and Nadia can be so difficult, I know. Sometimes I wanted to get back to you, and she would say that—'

'You need not tell me,' I broke in. 'I know without your telling me.'

Nina was on the verge of tears.

'But I have not really changed, Katia. You are just like a sister to us. I do love you.'

I kept staring at the lime-tree.

'You say so now because we are by ourselves. Next year, when Nadia is at Trostnikovo, you will play the same game again. Kolia was right about you—you are a weathercock.'

Now Nina was crying.

'Oh, Katia, no. I do promise, I do, I do—'

My indifference melted like a lump of ice under the sun. She was still the same Nina, we were back home, and I flung my arms around her neck. Never again were we to feel distant from each other.

That very happy, tranquil year flew on wings, and another spring came—slightly shadowed by the prospect of Nina, Volodia and their parents going to spend the entire summer in the Caucasus. Aunt Marie's health had certainly improved, but the doctors still insisted that the Caucasian waters would do her good. At the very end it was decided that Nastia should accompany them.

In those days the Caucasus did not wholly belong to Russia, and fighting was going on practically all the time here and there. To make matters even more hazardous, armed brigands from the south often came up north, attacked private carriages and even army convoys. We children knew about it since quite a few friends in the neighbourhood had lost relatives in such a way. Uncle Nicholas laughed and assured us that he would have a whole regiment to guard his wife and children on their way to Kislovodsk, but Nadia and I were dreadfully anxious.

'Those Circassians carry daggers, don't they?' I asked Nina.

'I think so, but, Katia, don't worry, please. If we do get attacked, well, so long as we are not left orphans—I mean I'd much rather they killed us all together.'

I shivered.

'They shan't,' I told her. 'But I know what you mean— not to be left an orphan. I would be if it were not for

Mamma.'

'Has your stepmother ever written to you?'

'No, nobody ever does—and I don't mind.'

'Don't you know anything about the wedding—why, nearly two years ago now, isn't it?'

'Mamma may have heard.'

'Cousin Sophie,' said Nina slowly, 'will never part with you.'

'Oh, I know, and even if Papa made me come, I would run away back to Trostnikovo—yes, all the way, on foot, just like that boy in the story *The Grey Coat.* You remember —he got home all right and he was much younger than I am.'

Presently Volodia and Nina, with their parents and Nastia, left for the wilds, and we welcomed Grand-maman and Nadia at Trostnikovo. Within a few weeks I realized that it was a Nadia I had not known before. Her manner softened, her arrogance lessened, she behaved at lessons and at games. Cousin Sophie's influence made itself felt from the very beginning, and little by little I grew quite attached to Aunt Marie's youngest sister.

Of course, I missed Nina dreadfully, but we were kept very busy and I had no leisure to brood over my friend's absence. Letters from the Caucasus reached Trostnikovo once a fortnight. Grand-maman and Cousin Sophie read and discussed them together, but those discussions never took place in our presence. Only from some hints dropped by Mademoiselle Berg did we learn that the waters were not doing Aunt Marie as much good as had been expected and she was longing to get back home.

'My dear child,' the governess always warned me, 'you must not mention any of it to Kolia.'

Our dear travellers came back on a wet September evening. Aunt Marie looked slightly thinner, otherwise there seemed no change in her. Volodia and Nina were bursting with health. They had so much to tell us about the Caucasus that Cousin Sophie at once granted us all a three-days' holiday. They had not seen any murderous Circassians, but the market at Kislovodsk, the veiled women, little girls decked out with silver and turquoise ornaments, the grim mountains, the rapidly running rivers, bread baked in the open and grapes sold by a sack, all of it suggested a world so entrancing and colourful that Nadia and I begged for more and more stories.

In October I had my eleventh birthday. I was now far less of a tomboy, and wild adventures in Kolia's company no longer tempted me. Nina complained that I did not chatter as much as I used to. I enjoyed our games as much as ever but books meant more and more to me.

We all knew it was our last year at Trostnikovo, and Cousin Sophie and I often talked about the future. She was determined to make me see Europe; she planned to go to Denmark, there to stay with my mother's relatives, and to Austria and Bavaria to present me to some very grand cousins of my father's Our travels were to end somewhere in Italy, where my adopted mother wanted to settle down.

Soon after my birthday Uncle Nicholas and Aunt Marie gave a big dinner at Trostnikovo. I cannot now remember why it was given, but it meant incredibly grand clothes for Nina and myself—fine white muslins with pale pink sashes and pink bows on the shoulders. I was very proud of Cousin Sophie's rich lilac satin gown trimmed with valenciennes. Fat Dasha, helped by another maid, had us all ready in good time, and we were waiting in the schoolroom for Mademoiselle Berg to take us downstairs when Aunt Marie came in. She was in palest blue with a toque of white plumes and silver, sapphires at her throat and wrists. So beautiful and radiant did she look, so exquisite was her dress that we all gasped with delight, and Kolia exclaimed:

'Mamma, you look every inch a queen! Anyone would pay court to you.'

'Anyone?' Uncle Nicholas echoed from the doorway. 'Well,

I like that, Kolia! Since when have you been calling your father "anyone"?'

Kolia blushed crimson and we all laughed. Many, many years have passed since that day but I still remember the glance Aunt Marie gave her husband. His own devotion fully matched her tenderness.

There were a great many guests at dinner. Nastia, Nadia, Nina and I, together with the boys and two handsome ensigns from a guards regiment, had a table to ourselves in a corner of the big dining-room. We joked and laughed so loudly that Cousin Sophie, her lilac skirts shimmering in the candle-light, left her place and came over to ask us to be a little less noisy. She looked most elegant, with the diamonds she wore so seldom in her ears and round her neck, but her face seemed rather flushed, and Nastia asked:

'Are you all right, Sophie?'

'Just a slight headache,' replied my adopted mother. 'I'll go upstairs after dinner, I think, but don't say anything to Grand-maman.'

Discipline and good manners forgotten, I jumped from my chair.

'Mamma.' The napkin slithered down to the floor. I looked frightened, but she smiled at me.

'Sit down at once. Only a bit of a headache—and on second thoughts I'll stay downstairs.'

I sat down again. I had such faith in her that the tranquil words made dust of my anxiety.

We had dancing after dinner and I promptly forgot all about Cousin Sophie and her flushed face. I had Volodia for the first quadrille and an elegant taciturn young man for my second partner. We four were allowed two dances only, but Nina and I hoped for the grace of a third before going up-stairs. According to the Trostnikovo régime, we had to ask permission from Cousin Sophie, and we could not see her anywhere, but even that did not make me anxious. I thought that she was probably in one of the drawing-rooms with Grand-maman and other elderly ladies, and I was just going to say to Nina 'I am going to find Mamma', when one of the doors of the ballroom opened and I saw old Lizbeth beckoning to me.

I rushed across to her.

'Mamma wants you,' she said in a whisper, 'and don't you fret, my dear. She is much, much better, and God is merciful.'

Panic swept over me. I wanted to run but my limbs would not obey me. Old Lizbeth took me by the hand and brought me to the breakfast-room. There were some people there. But I did not see them. I saw Cousin Sophie half lying in a deep armchair, her face ashen and her eyes closed. And I saw Dr. Nikolaev busily bandaging one of her wrists.

'Mamma—' my voice shook.

She opened her eyes and smiled at me.

'Don't worry, darling. I am feeling much, much better.'

But she at once closed her eyes again, and Aunt Marie put her arm about my shoulders. From a distance I heard Uncle Nicholas give an order. Footmen appeared and carried Cousin Sophie up the great staircase to her room. I followed behind, stumbling at every step, my eyes blinded by hot tears. Dr. Nikolaev and others began settling Cousin Sophie in her bed. On the outside landing Aunt Marie explained that my adopted mother needed absolute quiet, and I schooled myself to stop crying. That night Uncle Nicholas went to his dressing-room, and his wife had me in her room. I knew that Mademoiselle Berg and Amalie, the housekeeper, were with Cousin Sophie and that the doctor had not gone back to his own house in the grounds. I knew no more than that, but once away from that landing I gave vent to my grief. Some sixth sense told me that my beloved adopted mother had been very near death that evening. And I was not wrong. She had had a stroke. Help immediately given had saved her—but I could not help asking myself, 'For how long?'

And yet all the appearances were against such dark suppositions. Cousin Sophie had never been ill in all her life, and within three weeks she had completely recovered, though Uncle Nicholas insisted on summoning a specialist from Kiev to Trostnikovo. His verdict was that Cousin Sophie should go south to Odessa for sea-bathing the following summer. When the doctor had gone, Cousin Sophie said she would not commit herself to any such plan.

'It would be such a waste of time and money if I feel as well as I do now,' she said.

And indeed anyone looking at her would not have believed that she had had a stroke. She took up all the threads again and never seemed tired. When Aunt Marie begged her not to exert herself so much, she said that illness alone excused laziness and that she was perfectly well, and Dr. Nikolaev confirmed it. But both he and the specialist from Kiev insisted on a diet, and my adopted mother hated the very idea of it. Nobody would have called her greedy, but she liked her food. Once, I remember, a game pie was served at dinner. Ivan the butler passed by Cousin Sophie's chair and a footman ran up with a dish of stewed sweetbreads. She refused it and demanded the pie. Ivan paused uncertainly. Uncle Nicholas said:

'No, Sophie. You know as well as I do that rich things are bad for you.'

'It is all nonsense,' retorted Cousin Sophie, and left the table.

We stared down at our plates. Grand-maman and Aunt Marie at once told Uncle Nicholas that no rich dishes should be ever served at dinner.

'It is unkind to tease her,' said Aunt Marie.

'Properly speaking, darling, Sophie should have nothing except clear soup and toast. Would you like us all to keep to the table of a desert hermit?'

However, nothing of the kind ever happened again. And I remember that the single lapse, if it might be so called, deepened my feeling for her.

One late afternoon in December we were all sitting and working in the drawing-room, listening to Cousin Sophie reading *Pickwick* to us. Suddenly Mirza came to announce that a big box had arrived—addressed to her.

'How odd! I am not expecting anything from anywhere.' She put down the book and went into the hall, all of us following her.

We saw an enormous wooden crate, a big label gummed to the lid. Cousin Sophie bent to read it and then turned to me.

'It is from your father.' She spoke in a strangely tautened voice. 'I suppose he has remembered that you had another birthday two months ago.'

I stared at the crate. I felt at once embarrassed and excited. My father had not sent me anything for more than five years.

The servants began hammering at the lid of the crate. When it was removed, we came nearer and saw a flat parcel wrapped in fine white paper and tied with red ribbon. A small label was hanging from it and Cousin Sophie read it aloud:

'A present to Katia from her new mother.'

She smiled wryly but made no comment, and I felt furious. How dare a stranger, whom I had never met, call herself my 'mother'? And when the wrappings fell away, I saw that it was a present a girl like Lili Lukanova might have expected— a dress of rose silk crêpe embroidered from top to toe. It was spread on the sofa, and I could not help admiring it, but I knew it was most unsuitable for a girl of eleven accustomed to very plain clothes.

Underneath lay a flat box containing a black lace mantilla for Cousin Sophie.

'I can just imagine how many eyes were ruined over it,' she said. 'Why, I would be ashamed to wear it.'

'But, Sophie,' said Nastia, 'they could not send you any rubbish. It is a lovely mantilla. The design is exquisite.'

102

'And do I need anything like it?' Cousin Sophie sighed.

There followed toys, picture books, and a workbox of tortoiseshell and mother-of-pearl.

'I can only suppose that he does not know what to do with his money,' said Cousin Sophie. And, truly, that workbox was hardly suitable for an eleven-year-old girl.

The rest was sweets—sixty pounds of sweets!—with lots of dolls, flowers, trumpets and clocks made of chocolate and sugar.

The rose crêpe dress must have been put aside somewhere. I never wore it at Trostnikovo. I cannot remember what happened to the rest of the things. I know I would have preferred a letter to that elegant workbox. I felt that all those things had been sent by a stranger whose very face I could not remember. A few days later I asked:

'Shall I write?'

'I have already written,' answered Cousin Sophie. 'The box was addressed to me.'

## 11 *Dear Aunt Marie . . .*

It was a severe but quiet winter. A lot of snow fell as usual, but having fallen, it stayed deep and crisp. However pale, the sun came out almost every day, and we were spared rough winds and blizzards. Every tree in park and garden looked like a bride, veiled and mantled in shimmering silver. Which was rather appropriate since that particular winter was marked by a very grand wedding in January. I cannot now remember the girl's name, but guests from several provinces were coming to her father's place near Kursk, and we got rather excited on hearing that a grand-duchess was expected to come.

Now Kursk was not particularly close to Trostnikovo. When the invitation arrived, both Grand-maman and Cousin Sophie begged Aunt Marie not to travel so far. Nastia being included in the invitation, they argued that she could perfectly well go by herself so long as her maid and two men-servants accompanied her, but Aunt Marie would not hear of it. She pointed out that she would run no risks of catching a cold if she travelled in a thickly hooded sledge, with warmed bricks at her feet. She promised to wear her enormous sable cloak and to have bearskin rugs all over her.

So in the end, she, Uncle Nicholas and Nastia began getting ready for the festivities. The day after the wedding there was to be a fancy-dress ball at Kursk. To give pleasure to us children, Aunt Marie put on the dress she had had made for the occasion. It was the national costume. She represented Tsarina Anastasia Romanova, the first wife of Ivan the Terrible, a gentle and saintly woman who, had she not died so young, would surely have done all she could to prevent her husband from earning that dreadful sobriquet.

When I saw Aunt Marie in a silver tissue *sárafan*, her *kókoshnik* embroidered all over with pearls and amethysts and the transparent white veil framing her lovely face, I felt that she and the good Tsarina had indeed much in common. In Aunt Maria, physical beauty was matched by crystal-like qualities of heart and soul. Even now, at the distance of so many years, I know there was not a single day at Trostni-kovo when we did not feel happier and better for her presence among us. Her gentleness shamed our naughtiness, our little distresses were healed by her smile and her voice, our various pleasures were deepened once she shared them.

So the three left for Kursk. Yet, for all the precautions taken, Aunt Marie returned with a cough. It was not very troublesome at first. Then it worsened and ended by racking her. Presently, a hectic spot appeared on each cheek, and even in the mornings her hands were dry and hot, and at last she took to her bed.

Dr. Nikolaev was an experienced country doctor—but in this instance he refused to rely on his own diagnosis, and Uncle Nicholas spared no expense in getting specialists from Kiev and even from Moscow. Everyone recommended a different remedy—and all of them were tried in turn—asses' milk, baths of special herbs, champagne early in the morning. But nothing seemed to be of much use. Her cough became less savage, but her weakness increased almost day by day. By the end of March poor Aunt Marie could no longer walk, and a special wheelchair was made for her.

We children saw her every day, and of course we were gripped by anxiety, but we tried conscientiously to follow Cousin Sophie's advice.

'You would not help Aunt Marie much by fretting about her,' she said. 'Of course pray for her morning and evening, and in between think of the future when she will be well again. Don't brood over today. Just fix your thoughts on tomorrow.'

So we prayed twice a day. Cousin Sophie composed a lovely short prayer in French asking the Holy Spirit to give the grace of His strength to Aunt Marie. Never did we discuss her illness among ourselves.

I remember that winter ended unexpectedly early that year, and the coming of spring seemed to whisper about a miracle. Day by day, Aunt Marie's cheeks were less hollow and her colour more natural. She began eating with appetite and her cough was almost gone. Presently, to our wild joy, she gave up using the wheelchair. A sofa was placed for her on one of the balconies. There she stayed for hours with a book or some needlework, and what a pleasure it was to bring her posies of wild flowers from the park. Uncle Nicholas ordered bushes of white lilac to be replanted in tubs and placed all over the balcony. Those May weeks were fragrant indeed in every sense. From time to time Aunt Marie appeared in the dining-room and sometimes gave us a little music after the meal. Of course, we knew that she could no longer sing—but it was heavenly to see her gaining strength almost every day.

So we reached the middle of May.

We never knew the real cause of it. We heard from Fat Dasha and old Lizbeth that early one morning Aunt Marie had gone out to look at some newly bedded-out plants in her little private garden at the back of the hothouses. It had rained hard the evening before and she must have forgotten to change her indoor shoes for stout boots. It may well have happened in some such way, I cannot tell, but one particularly lovely May morning we found the sofa untenanted. Nina and the boys were in great distress. We went indoors— but Cousin Sophie stopped us at the head of the stairs and said we must not disturb Aunt Marie that morning. Later, her own maid told Fat Dasha that the mistress had coughed blood in the night.

Nastia gave us our French and geography lessons that morning. We never saw Cousin Sophie or Uncle Nicholas that day, and Mademoiselle Berg proved her sterling qualities to the full. She took us out of doors for the rest of the lessons. She so arranged the day that we were not left either idle or alone for a moment. Our dinner and supper were served to us in the schoolroom.

It was next morning that we heard Aunt Marie was most gravely ill—but, of course, we knew it already. Dr. Nikolaev was sleeping in the house. All the passages, stairs and landings at Trostnikovo were thickly carpeted but everybody glided about on tiptoe.

That day another doctor arrived. Inflammation of the brain was diagnosed. Aunt Marie lay mostly unconscious. When she came round, she recognized nobody. She laughed and screamed, and music alone could calm her. At once a piano was brought into an adjoining room, and Cousin Sophie and Nastia took turns in playing softly by the hour.

In our own wing we just lived from day to day. We saw nothing of Cousin Sophie who devoted herself wholly to our dear invalid, nor did Uncle Nicholas ever come near us. It fell to Mademoiselle Berg and Nastia to keep us as busy as was possible. We spent all our leisure hours reading aloud to Grand-maman, who must have been shaken to the depths but who kept her faith and courage to the end, and it made me happy to see the expression of her beautiful grey eyes whenever she watched Nadia and me together.

Every morning old Lizbeth came into our bedroom, delivered a brief and usually non-committal report, added, 'God is merciful, children,' and vanished without giving us time to ask a single question.

One morning in mid-June Cousin Sophie appeared in the schoolroom when we were having our German lesson, and we were so startled that the pens fell out of our hands and poor Nina broke into sobs.

'Is it—is Mamma—Cousin Sophie?' Kolia asked, his lips

white.

'She has come round, children. She wants to see you. You will be taken to her room in the afternoon.'

That, of course, marked the end of our German lesson. It was raining so hard that a walk was out of the question Nadia, Nina and I took out our needlework. The boys tried to get busy with something or other. We hardly spoke. We could not help our tears. I remember Fat Dasha's red and swollen face when she staggered in with our luncheon tray. We could not even look at the food and Mademoiselle Berg did not urge us.

I think we managed not to cry when Uncle Nicholas came in and we were taken into Aunt Marie's room. Nobody had said anything to us, but we knew we were being summoned to receive her last blessing, and quite by instinct we all knelt on coming in. Presently I raised my head, and I was shocked to see that anyone could have changed so much within a mere five weeks. All the beauty had gone. Hair cropped, eyes clouded, lips cracked, Aunt Marie looked old and tired beyond all telling. Everything about her seemed grey and spent, and I clutched my hands together under the pinafore and said to myself that I must not cry until I had gone from the room.

Old Lizbeth handed Aunt Marie a small icon in a gold frame. With an infinite effort she made the sign of the cross over us all. Then she said very slowly, her voice tautened:

'Well, children, God bless you ... Be happy ... Pray for me.'

One by one, we tiptoed up to the bed and kissed her poor thin hand. Then she leant back on the pillows. We were at once taken away. Once outside, the urge to cry left me altogether, and Nina, too, was very quiet.

Next morning we were told that Aunt Marie had received the last sacraments at dawn. Very quietly but firmly Mademoiselle Berg insisted on our having some breakfast, and we struggled with milk and rolls as much as we could. There were no lessons that day. All of us, including Cousin Sophie, gathered in Grand-maman's room. We did not talk. We waited, and the summer rain kept beating against the window-panes.

Suddenly a door slammed somewhere down a passage. We stayed dumb but we all looked at one another. The house had been so very still. In a few moments Uncle Nicholas came into the room, his face as white as chalk. He knelt by Grand-maman's sofa and said brokenly:

'Marie is gone.'

I saw his shoulders shake and I saw his mother-in-law put a trembling hand on his head. My poor little cousins seemed stunned. Then with a cry—'Papa, Papa'—they rushed to their father. I was clasped in Cousin Sophie's arms. Nastia and Nadia knelt by a window-sill, their faces buried in their hands. Nobody spoke for a long time. Nobody noticed the passing of the summer shower and the deep golden June sunshine rippling over the Turkey carpet and the old mahogany furniture. We stirred when the sad tones of the church bells were carried across the park.

According to the old Russian custom, all of us paid our last homage to Aunt Marie the next day. All in white satin, she lay, white flowers garlanding her head, weariness and torment gone from her face. Four tall candles, their sticks draped with black crêpe, stood at each of the four corners. A deacon stood at the foot of the coffin reciting the appointed psalms. The three windows were flung wide open. A bee was buzzing somewhere. I saw a robin perch on a bough of an oak and I smelt the first roses.

One by one we went up, knelt for a brief prayer, and kissed Aunt Marie's hand for the last time. Volodia and Kolia were crying very quietly, but Nadia and I between us had to lead poor Nina back to the door. And on the landing outside we saw little Liza running about, clapping her fat little hands and wanting her mother to see her new pink frock. Fat Dasha ran up and carried the child away to the nursery.

We were not taken to the funeral. Immediately it was over, Uncle Nicholas left to spend a few weeks by himself on his Chernigov estate, and Cousin Sophie began getting ready for her journey down to the Black Sea.

I had rather hoped that she would take me with her, and my hopes rose when I heard that Nastia was going with her. I had never seen the sea, and it seemed the most natural thing for me to be together with Cousin Sophie. Quietly and tenderly she explained why it would be better for her to leave me at Trostnikovo. Aunt Marie's illness and death were taking their toll.

'I am not as ill as they imagine—' Cousin Sophie referred to the doctors—'but, in all honesty, I feel a bit tired. If you came with me to Odessa, well, I would not get all the rest I need. I don't mean that you would worry me—but I would certainly have to devote some time to you, and I am told the treatment does eat into the day. You do understand? There will be frequent letters, my little daughter, and I know you won't forget to keep your diary, so that when I get back I shall know all you have been doing during my absence. I know you will be good—as you have been for so long, and prove that you can stand on your own feet. Once I am back, I want to start teaching you English and Italian. You must have at least a smattering of Italian before we settle down in Italy, and that won't be very long, darling. Uncle Nicholas thinks his boys will go to Kiev next spring. So, before another year is out, you and I will be travelling together.'

I listened to it all. I knew that my adopted mother was talking sense and I tried most valiantly not to cry the morning she left Trostnikovo in a south-bound coach.

She and Nastia were away for nearly three months. It was a very hot summer, and Mademoiselle Berg gave us all our lessons out of doors—in the garden, the orchards, the park, and even in the fields. In broad terms, it was rather a natural history summer for us. Trees and flowers, birds and insects, were her main themes. A wasps' nest, quite casually stumbled on, led to a talk about them. A visit to a son of an old cook, who kept bee-hives at the edge of a wood, resulted in a lecture on bee-keeping. And I still remember the poetic legend, *Fiedelhänschen*, with which Mademoiselle Berg ended one particularly interesting afternoon. It was the story about a fiddler-boy who had wandered into an enchanted wood. Whenever he played his fiddle, the music was echoed by harebells and forget-me-nots, by beeches and limes, together with nightingales, robins and thrushes, accompanied by a stream.

We missed Aunt Marie terribly, and little Liza's incessant questions were heart-breaking. She often stood by a window and watched the drive for the carriage to come up to the porch—for on however long a journey people went, they always came back. She must have thought some such thing. We missed Aunt Marie, but wounds get healed in childhood. The day came when we stopped crying on our frequent visits to the little chapel in the churchyard. We continued taking posies there, choosing always white and blue flowers for them, the two colours Aunt Marie had preferred to all others.

One late afternoon in August we five were playing ball in the great courtyard when we heard dogs barking furiously by the gate, and turning, saw some six or seven women pilgrims, in dusty black cloaks, with crooks in their hands, come in and turn to the left where the kitchens were.

In the old days, when Uncle Nicholas's mother was mistress, Trostnikovo used to be a veritable sanctuary for all such pious folk, and some of them, so I heard old Lizbeth say, would stay for weeks in a remote wing of the house. They always brought stories of miracles and portents, and talked most vividly about their wanderings from one ancient shrine to another.

But Uncle Nicholas did not like pilgrims and they stopped coming. That day in August they must have heard in the

111

village about his absence from home and hoped that old Lizbeth would befriend them for old times' sake. We stopped playing and watched them from a distance. I must confess that we rather shared Uncle Nicholas's dislike of them: the very few pilgrims we would meet in the neighbourhood always scared us with their gloomy prophecies of disasters soon to overtake the country.

Suddenly one of the black-cloaked women left her friends and made straight towards us.

'And which among you is Katia?' she asked.

I stepped forward. I did not recognize her—though the small, furtive eyes, the sharp nose and the jutting-out chin seemed all faintly familiar.

'Dear one,' she went on in a thin, sing-song voice, 'and have you forgotten your old Agatha?'

I tried to show pleasure at seeing her. I felt none at all. Nannie Agatha was just like a ghost out of a past I had wholly forgotten and had no wish to be reminded about. Yet, Cousin Sophie having trained me in common civility, I asked:

'And how did you find me here, Nannie?'

'Ah, dear one, God is merciful to pious folk,' she replied. 'I have been to so many shrines and fetched up at Sevsky Abbey—where their grandmother is'—here she gave a sugared smile to the others—'and the kind old lady told me how to get to you.'

'And have you come from Tver?' I asked reluctantly.

'Well, some months ago it will be now, dear one. You will have heard of little Varia?'

I stared at Agatha.

'Who is she?'

'Why, your half-sister, dear one, born nearly six months ago, but so ailing—they all say she won't live long.'

'I am sorry,' I murmured quite insincerely.

'Well, dear one, why should you be? What is she to you? Now there is Andrew, in his seventh year he is, and gone so naughty, too, and your old nannie, dear one, tried to train him properly—but the stepmother would not hear of it, and so there I was—asked for my papers and left them, and I mean to go back to Sevsky Abbey and end my days there, dear one. No room in the world for your old nannie—see?' She shook her black-capped head. 'The world is indeed cruel —but the end is in sight, praise be to the Lord.'

Agatha had not been a pilgrim for very long but she was perfectly at home in their curious and sombre conversation, and Nina and I secretly hoped that she would not stay long at Trostnikovo.

Grand-maman, having seen us from her window, sent for me and said:

'As she is your old nannie, Katia, tell her that she can stay here for a few days only—and no longer. Uncle Nicholas is expected home at the end of the week.'

Agatha did not wait for the invitation to be repeated. She carried her bundle into the house and soon enough found her way into our bedroom. By then, I must confess, my reluctance at meeting her again had given way to curiosity about my family.

And Agatha, whose loquaciousness was just the same as ever, had quite a lot to tell—but always in her own way, evading answers to awkward questions, adding cryptical comment to most ordinary statements, and colouring everything with a pilgrim's conviction that the world was too bad to live in and that one's only chance to escape from its evils was to hide one's self in a monastery, none of which said anything either to Nina or to myself.

'And your uncle is dead, dear one.'

I gasped. I had no idea I ever possessed an uncle, and said so.

'Well, that evil one,' replied Agatha. 'No wonder nobody had ever told you of him. Least said, soonest mended, and the estate is your papa's now—but he won't live there, and no wonder! But your stepmamma brought him a big house

113

in Tver and another estate—so all is well with them, I reckon. A cheese and butter life, dear one, I can tell you.'

'What about my stepmother?' I ventured to ask.

'Well, young and beautiful she is—but far too soft with Andrew. And she talked to me a lot about you, dear one, before I left them. She said, "Go and find her, Agatha," she said. "Tell her I love her—her cousin won't give her up, I hear," she said, "but I do want to see her—I hear that she is very clever and knows such a lot." Yes, dear one, that is how it is—and there is plenty of this world's goods coming to you, but they won't help you get to the Lord.'

At last Mademoiselle Berg decided that Agatha had talked more than enough, and old Lizbeth was summoned to take her away.

Agatha's unexpected arrival had certainly excited me. But I did not feel in the least disturbed. All her conversation seemed to concern itself with strangers I was unlikely to meet. I kept saying to myself:

'I belong to Mamma, and she will soon be back, soon, soon, soon.'

## 12 *The end of Trostnikovo for Katia*

Uncle Nicholas was away most of that summer. From Chernigov he went to Kiev, and then on to St. Petersburg. He wrote to us all regularly and we knew when to expect him home. When he returned, we were struck by the change in him. He stooped a little, was much thinner, very quiet in his manner, and there were deep lines about his mouth and silver streaking his black hair. His children and I welcomed him most boisterously, but his old vivacity had gone. No guests now came to Trostnikovo, and Uncle Nicholas spent most of the time either in the fields or in the estate office. His leisure was divided between Grand-maman and us children, but no games were ever suggested at such times, and Kolia, who sometimes accompanied his father on horseback, told us that Uncle Nicholas would ride for an hour without saying one word.

Yet he was just as kindly and tender with us as before.

Post from Odessa came every Saturday; there was always something for me in the package and long letters for Uncle Nicholas and Grand-maman. Occasionally he would bring a letter into the schoolroom and read it aloud. Very often we noticed him skip a whole page. Later I would try to wheedle it out of him, but I never succeeded. Many years were to pass before those letters came into my hands, and I understood why Uncle Nicholas kept so much of their contents to himself. Apparently poor Cousin Sophie was already convinced that her journey to Odessa had been a mistake and that sea-bathing was doing her more harm than good. 'Should I die suddenly here in the south, I know I can trust you, dear Nicholas, to do the best possible for my dear little daughter.'

She and Nastia returned in September. That afternoon Mademoiselle Berg and all of us happened to be in a field adjoining the high road, and Kolia was the first to see the carriage turning in at the gates. At once I raced back to the house, shedding my sun-bonnet and a shoe on the way. I found Cousin Sophie alone in the breakfast-room, and what did I not feel at seeing that dear face again? I believe I cried, and then I began talking nonsense, so anxious was I not to let her see that I noticed the change in her. Her grey-blue eyes were sunk and I could feel her bones under the thin stuff of her travelling dress. The hand that caressed me was so thin that she no longer wore her rings.

'Mamma, Mamma, such a lot to tell you!'

'I know, my joy, but later. I am going to tell them to prepare a bed for you on the sofa in my bedroom, and we shall have the whole evening by ourselves.'

When Cousin Sophie got up, I noticed that she moved with difficulty, but I said nothing and thought she was probably very tired after the journey.

I had to share her with Grand-maman and all the others till the evening. At last we were in her room. Her maid came in to help her undress.

'Just this once, Olga,' said Cousin Sophie, 'will you please help me get my shoes and stockings off? My feet feel quite wooden.'

Olga knelt and very carefully took off the shoes and stockings. A chill ran down my spine and I could hardly smother a cry of horror: Cousin Sophie's feet and legs were terribly swollen and bandaged from the ankle to the knee.

She smiled at me whilst Olga was brushing her hair.

'See what a crock of a mother you have got, dearest? Now I shall sit in a chair all day long and you will take care of me and work hard at your lessons and be good.'

I brushed the tears away from my eyes and promised most

fervently. Whatever the state of her health, it was such happiness to have her back and to know that we would never be parted again!

Olga went. Cousin Sophie's ermine-lined bedjacket over my shoulders, I scrambled on to her bed, and started on my vast chronicle—my great friendship with Nadia, our games with little Liza, my progress in German and history, Mademoiselle Berg's 'nature' lessons—'we have learned so much about ants and bees and wasps, Mamma.' Into that breathless narrative I sandwiched questions about Odessa and its climate, its people, and the Black Sea. Were there many Tartars there? Was she ever going back, and would we travel together next time?

Cousin Sophie listened and did not interrupt, something of a sad smile playing about the corners of her mouth. Probably she was rather astonished that never once did I ask about the result of the treatment. In all truth, I was afraid to ask such a question. When I stopped to draw a badly needed breath, she patted my knee with her emaciated hand and said in a low voice:

'I fear, dearest, that you and I are unlikely ever to travel together. It seems that God does not wish me to finish your education. Probably He has other plans for you.'

Dumb for once, I stared at her, my mouth shaking. She pressed me to her breast.

'Don't let us discuss my tiresome illness, dearest. I'll tell you all about it some time. I see that you have kept your promise and worked harder than ever. I do thank you, my joy—nothing could have pleased me more. Now is there anything else?'

'Yes.' I spoke dully. 'Agatha came here on her way to Sevsky Abbey. You remember her, Mamma? My old nurse. She wants to become a nun now. And oh, I did not know that I had a sister and an uncle. He is dead.'

'He was your father's elder brother,' explained Cousin Sophie.

117

'Did you know him, Mamma?'

'Yes, in the old days. He never married and lived all by himself and went nowhere. He was a very unhappy man, Katia, and had no use for anyone, I am afraid.'

'Was he evil, Mamma?'

'Certainly not. Whatever put that into your head?'

'Agatha said he was.'

'Oh, these Russian peasants,' sighed Cousin Sophie. 'They think that anyone not of their religion is necessarily bad. Your Uncle Adalbert remained a Catholic, darling, and your father turned Orthodox. But your uncle was not an evil man at all. He just lived a hermit's life—and I happen to know that he did quite a lot of good—without too many people knowing anything about it.'

'Papa never mentioned him to me,' I said slowly.

'Your father did not see eye to eye with him—but they had never quarrelled.'

I thought hard.

'Mamma, before Nadia and I became friends, she would often mock at me for being a foreigner.'

'She should never have mocked, darling, but it is true— your father being what he is and your mother being a Dane. But you were born in Russia, and don't forget that all nations are the same in God's sight.'

'Not, surely, those in Africa?'

'All over the world, dearest,' said Cousin Sophie. 'Do you imagine that, having made white men, God let someone else create them black and yellow? And now it is time to sleep.'

I slept soundly enough. But in the morning my adopted mother could not leave her bed—so swollen were her feet. Only towards dinner-time was I able to pilot her into the dining-room where an armchair and a footstool had already been arranged for her.

Dr. Nikolaev thought that a simple milk cure might do some good. Certainly, within a fortnight of her return Cousin

Sophie felt much stronger and her poor legs troubled her much less. Of course, she could no longer shoulder any of her old tasks. Nastia and Mademoiselle Berg between them now taught Nadia and Nina, and a tutor was engaged for the boys until the spring when they were going to a school in Kiev. I remained Cousin Sophie's only pupil, and practically lived in her room.

She continued teaching me, her mental energy and verve unaffected by her illness. She did more than that. All thought of self tossed aside, she began—day by day—to prepare me for a future without her. Very, very gradually she made it plain to me that—once she was gone—I would have to leave for Tver. When for the first time the idea found lodgment in my mind, I felt sick with despair, since life without her seemed a shadowy wilderness, and I believe it was the very last occasion when I cried in her presence. Little by little, however, Cousin Sophie succeeded in persuading me that I had a family and a roof-tree of my own. Stoically objective, she went to discuss my father's second marriage from a point of view I found altogether novel. She admitted that she had been against it at the beginning.

'It was just the memory of your own mother, dearest. But I have since heard much about your stepmother, and she seems as good as she is beautiful. Certainly, she has made your father very happy.'

'And what would I have to call her?' I mumbled, my face turned towards the window. Cousin Sophie's voice never faltered as she answered:

'You will call her "Mamma" and you will ask God to make you love her.'

That evening, I remember, I went to our bedroom and buried my face in the pillow. Nina at once tried to comfort me, but I could share none of it with her. Those conversations with Cousin Sophie were something of an enclosure where none might enter except our two selves.

One evening in late October Cousin Sophie said to me:

119

'Listen, Katia. Materially you are well provided for since I am leaving you all I have. Your father will probably send you to some good boarding-school in Moscow, but no school, however excellent, can end anyone's education. Never say to yourself, "I know enough," and never be afraid of hard work. And remember that God is your constant helper and guide. Were it not for my faith in Him, I would truly lose heart that I am leaving you without the happiness of seeing you grown-up, my dearest little daughter.'

She went on talking but, for no rhyme or reason, my thoughts wandered off. I suddenly remembered a box made of cut glass tinted yellow and dark green where Cousin Sophie kept her jewellery—some emerald and ruby rings, a string of garnets, a few bracelets, and her diamonds which she hardly ever wore—a ring, two brooches, a hair ornament and a necklace.

'Why, all these things will be mine,' I thought, staring aimlessly at the tongues of blue-orange flame leaping in the fireplace, and Cousin Sophie's voice broke in:

'Katia, I believe you are not listening at all.'

I blushed a wild crimson, whole-heartedly ashamed of myself.

'And what were you thinking of?'

'Mamma, don't ask me,' I begged her, 'because I could not fib to you.'

'No,' she said musingly, 'all your little fibs were so unconvincing, and your face always betrayed you at once. I remember years ago you looked like a frightened little owl.'

Things worsened sharply just before Christmas. Cousin Sophie's legs were now so swollen that she could no longer leave her bed, and her hands, too, were affected so that writing was beyond her, and I became her little secretary, writing letters in three languages, to her dictation, of course.

I still shared a bedroom with Nadia and Nina, and Cousin Sophie insisted on my getting adequate exercise whenever the weather allowed it. Otherwise, I lived wholly in her room, and meals were served there. Nastia, Nadia and Nina came every evening to wish her goodnight, Grand-maman sent daily messages, and Uncle Nicholas came two or three times a week. Volodia and Kolia I did not see at all except sometimes in the garden. It was truly a hermit's life, but I did not see it as such. I grudged every moment spent away from Cousin Sophie.

Some time in January Uncle Nicholas left Trostnikovo, and I think it was old Lizbeth who contrived to send a message to Agatha at Sevsky Abbey to come to us. Cousin Sophie had never much cared for my old nurse—but now she seemed glad of her, and Agatha, well accustomed to look after invalids, proved herself invaluable in making Cousin Sophie as comfortable as possible.

In early February she felt better. The condition of her hands improved to the extent of her being able to wield the pen again, and it made me almost delirious with joy to see how pleased Dr. Nikolaev was with her. About a week later, when the girls came to say good night, Cousin Sophie turned to Nadia:

'Kiss dear Grand-maman for me, my friend, and tell her that if tomorrow I feel as well as today, I will ask them to wheel my chair to her room. I do so want to see her. Good night. God bless you all.'

They were all gone. And now it was my turn. I climbed on to the bed, and she took my face in both hands and smiled at me:

'I do like you with your hair loose. And how much more tranquil you are! You used to be such a cry-baby! Well, my joy, will you kiss me in the old way—you know—prove that it doesn't make you sick to caress your useless old mamma.'

For answer, I flung my arms round her neck and covered

her face with my kisses. Then she murmured:

'Now go to bed and God bless you, my little daughter.'

I turned at the door. Cousin Sophie's eyes were on me, a look so full of love that I hurried away not to disturb her by my tears.

I woke to a grey wintry morning to see Nina, her face buried in the pillow, and old Agatha standing at the foot of my bed.

'Get up, child,' she said solemnly, 'and say a prayer for the repose of the soul of God's servant Sophie.'

But I did not get up. I stared and then cried:

'And I was not there, I was not there! Why didn't some-one fetch me?'

In a moment they were all round my bed—Mademoiselle Berg, Nastia, Nadia, Fat Dasha, Olga and Amalie the house-keeper. Cousin Sophie had not been left alone, they told me in turn. Nastia had come at midnight to find her asleep; Mademoiselle Berg had looked in at two in the morning to find her awake but comfortable and wanting a drink of water. Two hours later it was Amalie's turn.

'She was asleep, child, and I did not wake her.'

Later that day Dr. Nikolaev told me that Cousin Sophie had died in her sleep towards dawn.

I found myself in a wilderness but I knew that she whom I loved above all others was at peace. I did not feel in the least frightened and spent the first night in the room where she lay. Still in my dark brown merino, I just huddled in a corner of the sofa from where I could see her face, and the big candles went on burning all through the night.

But there was something very strange. Six years of close affectionate companionship with my little cousins were as though they had never been. They all exerted themselves to comfort me, but even Nina seemed remote, and when we were together, I found I had nothing to say to her. The idea that my days at Trostnikovo were numbered neither excited nor disturbed me. The day after the funeral I developed a temperature, and Dr. Nikolaev kept me in bed for about a fortnight. I do not think I was really ill but I felt as weak as though everything inside me were straw and hay. Nastia, Nadia and Nina went in and out of the room. I may have been glad of their visits—I cannot remember. Agatha washed me, did my hair, brought my meals, and mouthed her pious platitudes, but I hardly listened to her.

Rather vaguely I supposed that my father would come and fetch me away. But he did not appear and nobody wrote to me. I waited, and I ended by waiting impatiently. Trostnikovo had meant Cousin Sophie to me from the very beginning. With her gone, the house became a shell tenanted by people I knew well and still loved—but now there stretched a gulf between us.

Not till the middle of May did I learn that one Madame von Giers, a friend of my stepmother's, was waiting for me at Kursk. Agatha got ready quickly enough. I said goodbye to everybody in turn. Most of them cried. I alone had no tears. I was in a hurry to get away. The past lay dead and I would not look at it.

# 13 *A new life*

It was a seven-hundred-mile journey. I think it lasted three weeks or even a little longer.

By the time Agatha and I came to Kursk, the first big town along our route, she and I had had more than enough of each other. The heat held, my head ached, my nerves were like frayed ribbons. I slept badly and refused all food except milk and wheaten rusks. To Agatha, I was just like a four-year-old in the nursery. She did not dare to spank me, but she scolded incessantly and she sneered. The first evening, when she heard me say my prayers in three languages, she permitted herself to say that she hoped life under my father's roof would soon turn me into 'a proper little Christian' in spite of all the obvious heathenry I had learned at Trost-nikovo. I lost my temper and reminded her that she was a servant and that I would complain to my father about her unkindness. The threat—which I would never have carried out—worked to a certain extent. Agatha refrained from scolding but went on grumbling all to herself. I ended by turning away from her.

For some reason or other we stayed quite a few days at Kursk, where Madame von Giers greeted me almost too effusively, such a honeyed smile on her lips that I felt as though too much sugar had been put into my tea. But that first impression did not last. Agatha, unpacking my night things, reported that I had been 'very naughty' on the journey. The plump little woman with rosy cheeks and dark brown eyes at once shook her head.

'Come, come, Nannie, have you forgotten how ill she has

124

been? Her Uncle Nicholas wrote and told me all about it.'

Agatha sniffed but did not dare make a retort. The moment should have filled me with a sense of triumph. It did not. I merely wanted to be alone. There seemed so much unnecessary noise in the wilderness to which Cousin Sophie's death had led me.

I am afraid Madame von Giers' kindness proved rather bad for me. The very next morning she stole a march on Agatha and came into my room to wash and dress me. I accepted her services with what good grace I could muster. Agatha did not believe her eyes when she saw that elderly lady put on my stockings and tie up my garters. At Trostnikovo Fat Dasha had long since been forbidden to help us with our dressing—we were big enough to manage on our own. But I had left Trostnikovo and I did not care.

'Dear one,' my old nurse began unctiously, 'it is not fitting that you should have your shoes put on for you.'

Madame von Giers finished with the garters and turned round.

'Oh, Nannie,' she spoke reproachfully, 'I am sure poor Katia is still very tired.'

Agatha retreated—this time without even a sniff, and I knew that in my stepmother's friend I had someone I could twist round my little finger.

We went on northwards, making a slight detour to a place called Korénna. I had never heard of it before. Madame von Giers explained that its church possessed a miraculous icon of Our Lady. I still did not understand why we should make that detour east.

'Well, Katia, I promised your people to stop there on the way home.'

'But why?' I asked coldly.

Agatha pursed her lips. Madame von Giers looked slightly bewildered.

'Well, it is a holy shrine, my dear, and a visit there might benefit your health. I am sure your poor head will stop

125

aching.'

I understood none of it, visits to shrines not having been part of my upbringing, but it seemed better to stop asking questions.

The farther we got from Kursk, the more crowded became the highway. The travellers were all pilgrims, many on foot, others on horseback, and the majority in all kinds of vehicles. Our own coach, drawn by four horses, overtook them all. Pilgrims on foot moved to the edge of the road, halted, and raised their staffs in greeting. They looked dusty, they were barefoot and their hair was dishevelled. They seemed so wild to me that I drew back from the open window, but Agatha kept now waving her hand, now crossing herself, and took to telling Madame von Giers all about the sanctuaries she had visited. I listened, half-wondering whether my old nurse had indeed been to so many places.

'Why, it sounds as though Agatha had worn a pair of seven-league boots,' I thought.

In her turn, Madame von Giers began describing all the great shrines she had seen. She talked so ardently that I began wondering whether the new world I was about to enter might not be some kind of a gigantic monastery. The idea did not please me at all, and—however fleetingly—a sharp longing for the restrained ways of Trostnikovo welled up in me.

In about four hours we reached the outskirts of Korénna, the horses having had to slow down their pace because of the crowds.

Korénna was a glorified hamlet rather than a town but it was famous, as I would learn later, all over the country because of its icon, and the annual fair with a turnover running into millions.

I liked the sprawling timbered inn, but the masses of singing, crying and shouting men and women milling up and down the only street and all round the church, terrified me so much that I burst into tears and begged to be taken back to the inn—but at Korénna Madame von Giers proved that she was not really a cushion for me to thump as I would. She held me firmly by the hand and led me on and on. Fortunately the ceremony of paying homage to the celebrated icon did not last long.

'Now I am sure your poor head is much better, Katia,' said Madame von Giers on our return to the inn.

It was not, but it would have been unkind to say so.

I cannot now remember what exactly delayed us at Korénna, but we did not leave until very late in the evening. The old innkeeper and his genial plump wife begged Madame von Giers to put off leaving till dawn. It appeared that the road beyond the pilgrims' camp was considered unsafe at night because of highwaymen. The postilion, however, assured my stepmother's friend that everything would be all right, that our horses were marvellous and the coachman wholly reliable. I heard all those conversations.

'Let us wait, please, let us wait,' I begged.

But Madame von Giers replied that far too many people were apt to talk nonsense about highwaymen. She said that she had often enough left Korénna late at night and nothing had ever happened to her.

So we left. The night air was most gratefully cool and everybody at Korénna seemed asleep. I was wrapped in several rugs and Madame von Giers begged me to lie down in my corner of our spacious hooded *brítchka,* but I refused to do so until we had passed 'the danger spot'.

Outside, well away from the main road, lay an immense plain dotted all over with white tents. Moonlight and the leaping flames of several bonfires gave it an almost unearthly quality. I heard voices from a distance, the barking of dogs and the neighing of horses, and shadows of people flickered between one tent and another. I asked if it was a gypsy camp.

'No, my dear,' Madame von Giers said comfortably. 'They are all pilgrims. There would be no room at Korénna for all

127

of them. So many arrive with their own servants and horses and settle down in the open air for three or four days.'

When the great camp lay well behind us, I thought I could settle down in my comfortable bed in a corner, when all suddenly we heard the galloping of horses far behind us. I sat up at once. I saw the coachman and the postilion cast a look back. Then the coachman gave a shrill whistle, and we were off . . .

I scrambled on to Madame von Giers' lap, my body shaking all over. Agatha began reciting prayers. We were galloping like mad. Both coachman and postilion urged the horses on and on, and they, as though aware of the danger, flew like birds.

'It is the highwaymen, the highwaymen,' I kept repeating.

Madame von Giers clasped me tight and begged me to place my trust in God, but in my imagination I already saw terrible, brutal faces, all burning eyes and tangled black beards, looking into the *brítchka*.

'God be merciful to thy servants,' said Agatha for about the tenth time, and I knew that Madame von Giers' heart was beating harder and harder. The villains were certainly gaining on us. We heard their wild shouts, and I closed my eyes for a second. Then suddenly in the far distance the head-lamps of the diligence making for Kursk gleamed steady and bright, and the pursuit at once slacked off. Something heavy, probably a stone hurled by one of the brigands, hit the hood of the *brítchka*. Then all was still. We were saved by the coachman's honesty and the truly wonderful horses.

I should here explain that brigandage had been the curse in Russia for centuries. All too often, alas, hired coachmen were known to work hand in glove with the highwaymen. They never attacked by daylight and their activities slackened in winter. I heard it said that side-lanes were as dangerous as a high road, particularly when they were fringed by trees. The robbers usually had their 'lairs' in the heart of some deep forest where neither police nor military dared to penetrate. When caught, they were dealt with severely enough, but no penalties, however grim, seemed strong enough to uproot the evil, and the luckless travellers who fell into their clutches were always killed on the spot to prevent the least information being laid against the brigands. At the time of my journey to Tver I was not acquainted with all those details, of course, but I knew quite enough for the mere sound of the word *razboynik* to make me shake in my boots.

As to the rest of that interminable journey, I remember it but patchily. Heat struck at the country without mercy, rivers ran shallow, and the sun was terrific. Not a day broke but my poor head ached worse and worse, and I would spend whole hours lying motionless in my corner. But I do remember a ghastly fire at Orel as we were driving through it, fields blackened by drought round about Tula, endless excursions of piety and shopping in Moscow. There were days when I was naughty, and Agatha, as I could well see, would be hard put to it to keep her temper. There were days when I behaved well, but Madame von Giers never changed. I was always her 'dear little Katia' no matter what I did, and her conversation was certainly far more informative than Agatha's.

I seldom, if ever, thought of Trostnikovo and of my little cousins whom I would never meet again. My thoughts were all on the future, and sometimes they were exciting and sometimes I felt troubled. I wanted to know everything about my stepmother. What colour were her eyes? Was she tall or small? Was she very strict about the house? Did she like singing and dancing? Had she ever been to school? It was satisfactory to learn that she was gentleness personified, that her eyes were violet-blue, that she was of middle height and possessed a lovely voice, and that she had spent a couple of years at a French finishing-school in Moscow.

'And your father, dear Katia, is very much thought of all over the province,' said Madame von Giers, but I showed a curious indifference either about him or my two brothers.

'You know that your little sister Varia died just before Christmas. She was a very sickly baby and nobody thought she would live long—but her grandmother was terribly upset.'

'Goodness,' I cried, 'so I have a new Grand-maman.'

Madame von Giers looked rather ill at ease.

'Well, yes, but she lives on her estate, some distance from Tver.' She hesitated. 'Dear Katia, I must warn you never to call her "Grand-maman". You see, little Varia was her *own* grand-daughter.'

'And what do I call her?'

'Oh, just Madame Khitrovó.' Madame von Giers made an effort to sound convincing: 'She is a very kindly old lady. I am sure you will love her, and your new mamma is her favourite daughter.'

I felt puzzled but I asked no further questions. I was sure, however, that I would not open my heart to 'the kindly old lady', who obviously looked upon her son-in-law's children as so many outsiders.

At last our *brítchka* drove through the Moscow toll-gate at Tver. I leant out of the carriage. I could not recognize either the street or the buildings, but I remembered that our house used to face the river and when the horses, having crossed the bridge, went straight on, I gasped:

'Aren't we going home now?'

Madame von Giers looked perplexed. Agatha explained hurriedly:

'The master sold the other house on his second marriage, dear one.'

In a few moments the *brítchka* drove into a large court-yard with a two-storied grey house at the end. Stables and outbuildings joined the two wings of the house. Beyond stretched an apparently immense garden. The courtyard teemed with servants, all of them strangers to me. Some-one helped me out of the carriage and I saw semi-circular steps leading up to the porch. The doors were wide open.

I was in a maze as I mounted the few steps and found myself in a light, spacious hall. At the end was a wide spiral staircase carpeted in dark blue. I saw four women on the first landing. They were all looking down into the hall and smiling at me.

In the middle stood a tall, majestic elderly lady, her hands folded on the silver knob of a cane. She wore a white gown trimmed with black lace and a cap with blue ribbons. On her left stood a pale young woman in deep mourning and close to her was a plump little body in brown, her cheeks very rosy and her eyes very bright. To the right of the tall lady in white I saw a young woman in a gown of pale green jackonet. Her plaited auburn hair was dressed into a coronet on her head. Both her look and her smile were irresistible.

'How can anyone be quite so beautiful?' I thought as I stood rooted at the bottom of the staircase.

'Katia, guess which of us is your new mother?' asked the tall lady in white.

I knew at once that she was Madame Khitrovó. I did not answer. I ran up the stairs towards the woman in pale green, and she opened her arms.

'My little one ... Alexis's own and mine. At last, at last,' she murmured, bending over me.

I was too dazed to speak. Nothing I had imagined was quite like that moment. My new mother took my sticky little hand and led me through a door. We sat down on a small brocade sofa in a corner of the ballroom, and I trembled from head to foot.

'Quietly, child, quietly,' she was saying, her hand stroking my head.

The other three ladies followed us.

'This is my mamma, Katia,' said my new mother, and I rose and ducked, trying to make a curtsy. Madame Khitrovó kissed me warmly enough, held my chin in her hand, and said rather severely:

'You must have her clothes changed at once, Elizabeth. A black woollen dress, a leather belt and what shoes! Dreadful! Anyone would take the child for a novice. What were those people thinking of?'

'Yes, yes,' replied my new mother, but I, coming out of my daze, raised my head and said clearly:

'I am in mourning for my mamma.'

'For your—' began Madame Khitrovó, when her daughter checked her at once.

'Now, Katia, this is my sister, Natalie, and that is her friend, Mademoiselle Catherine Eulaguina.'

The woman in mourning and the plump little body in brown both kissed me in turn. We were still in the ballroom, my new mother's hand in mine, and I was again wondering if I were awake or not. I had never expected to find myself so *wanted*. Presently a crowd of servants trooped into the ballroom and, to deepen my confusion, all of them kissed my hand. A lanky dark-haired boy of thirteen, wearing an unfamiliar uniform, appeared from behind the sofa, clicked his heels, and kissed me rather hurriedly on the cheek. He was Nicholas, but I would never have recognized him. Through a doorway waddled a plump, red-cheeked seven-year-old in a blue linen smock and white pantaloons. He panted up to the sofa, stood on tiptoe, licked my cheek with his tongue, and then waddled away as fast as he could. It was Andrew, whom I could only remember as a baby in his cot.

'Where is Papa?' I asked rather anxiously.

'He will soon be here,' someone answered, and we went into another room. I saw Madame von Giers and smiled at her. Agatha, of course, vanished to the back regions.

Tea came. My new mother had just poured thick cream into my cup when I seized her hand.

'I am sorry... I am not allowed cream.'

Madame Khitrovó at once turned to me.

'Who does not allow you cream?'

'I have never been given it at home.'

'Your home, my dear, is here,' she said severely. 'If your mamma has put cream into your tea, it means that you can drink it.'

My lips trembled. Madame von Giers at once came to my rescue.

'They told me that fat is bad for Katia.'

'Those foreign ideas,' bristled Madame Khitrovó, but I saw my stepmother fill another cup and put a slice of lemon into it, and I felt quietened.

Suddenly there were quick steps outside.

'It must be Alexis,' cried my stepmother, her eyes shining like sapphires.

The door was flung open. I sat motionless. I stared. A tall and handsome stranger stood there. Some inner voice kept whispering: 'Get up, run to him, he is your father,' but I sat still.

'Katia, don't you know me?'

In an instant he lifted me off my chair, his arms held me tight, his lips were on my cheeks and eyes.

'The very image of her mother,' he said almost under his breath. He lowered me back into the chair and, without looking at anyone, left the room, not to appear again that day.

'What an Englishman of a husband you have got, Elizabeth,' said Madame Khitrovó in a mocking voice. 'Not to have seen his daughter for six years and to behave so oddly!'

My stepmother flushed but said nothing, and how fervently did I hate Madame Khitrovó at that moment! It was a great pleasure to me when, tea finished, her carriage was announced, and she, her daughter, Natalie, and Mademoiselle Eulaguina left for the country.

# 14 *It all was rather puzzling at first . . .*

It was my thinness that led to a host of remarks and conjectures on the part of my new relations. I had never been plump in my life and, naturally, neither my illness nor the long journey would have put much flesh on my bones. But before that first day was over, my stepmother and her sister Natalie were wondering whether to send for a doctor. To my great relief, that decision was postponed.

'Now, careful, careful, Katia,' said my stepmother when we reached the three or four steps leading into the garden. 'Hold on to the banisters.'

'I can jump down,' I said, did so, and laughed.

She shook her head.

'You might have twisted your ankle.'

'I can climb trees and railings,' I told her, 'and run terribly fast.'

She kept shaking her head.

'Yes, and once you had a terrible accident,' she reminded me. 'I would not have a moment's peace if I knew you were climbing trees.'

From that first day I discovered that I was supposed to be dependent on servants for the least service. My stepmother would no more have thought of putting on her stockings than hiring a carriage to go to the moon. That very first evening, brought by her to my room, I smiled at the young pink-cheeked Masha, appointed to be my maid, and told her I would not need her services. My stepmother said nothing and waited for the girl to leave the room.

'Katia, dearest, who is going to undress you and plait your

134

hair?'

'I have done it myself for five years,' I told her. 'Fat Dasha was allowed to hook our dresses at the back and do our hair occasionally.'

'Surely they could not have been short of servants at Trostnikovo?'

'The house teemed with them,' I replied, plying my brush, 'but we were expected to do as much as we could ourselves.'

My stepmother made no comment. She watched me undress, fold up my clothes very neatly on a chair, pour the water from a big jug into the basin, and wash in cold water from head to foot.

'But, surely, you had hot water in the winter?' she asked at last.

I shook my head.

'Only when we had tubs—once a week—and none of us ever had a cold.'

She looked more puzzled than ever. I knelt to say the accustomed prayers in three languages. She waited for me to finish and get into bed before she said:

'We did not do it even at Madame Genlis's. How odd, dearest, to address your God in an alien tongue.'

I was not yet twelve. The long journey lay behind me. I realized perfectly that I was at home. She had attracted me from the first moment, I longed to win her love wholly, and then and there I decided that I would make as few allusions as possible to Trostnikovo and its ways. I could well see that the latter seemed incomprehensible and foreign to my stepmother and her world. And, as I was to learn later, it would have been wiser to keep to my resolve.

She hesitated briefly and then sat down in a chair by my bed.

'It must all seem strange to you,' she began.

I could not very well tell her that I loathed Madame Khitrovó. I took refuge in remarking:

'Well, I am not used to all that hand-kissing. At Trostnikovo servants were never allowed to do it.'

'But it is a very old custom,' she murmured, and went on
hurriedly: 'Darling, I do hope you will be happy among us.
What did you think of your brothers?'

I thought hard for a moment.

'Well, I have not seen much of Nicholas—he seems rather
serious for his age, doesn't he? Andrew is adorable and
what a baby—for all he is nearly seven.' Here I leant forward. 'But there is you. You are Papa's wife and my new
mother.' And impulsively I added, 'Mamma.'

'My dearest,' she murmured.

Those first days in my father's house were like so many
birthdays. Not a visitor came to the house but had a present
for me. I was caressed and petted all day long, and my
wishes and preferences were consulted at every turn. Did I
like the ornaments in my room? Were the curtains thick
enough to exclude the sun? Was there enough shelf-room
for my books? Though here my stepmother expressed a hope
that I would not spend too much time over them—I needed
a good long holiday after my illness. Had Agatha been there,
she would have grumbled, scolded and interfered, but my
stepmother had no use for Agatha, who had left on one of
her pilgrimages the very day after my arrival.

Even Madame Khitrovó proved something of a chame-
leon: she reappeared soon after with her daughter, Natalie,
and brought an enormous box of toys for me. Of her sharp-
ness and sternness there was not a sign. She was all solici-
tude.

'Little Katia,' she declared to my stepmother, 'must do
nothing but eat, sleep and amuse herself. That might put
colour into her cheeks and some flesh on her bones. She is
like a skeleton and wax could not be paler. Now, Elizabeth,
you are coming to Dubky in July and then going on to your
own place, I hear. I wanted you at Dubky for a whole month,
but your husband would not hear of it.'

'Mamma, Alexis has so much to do on the estate.'

'He will always find excuses,' said Madame Khitrovó. 'However, the child will spend the summer in the country.'

'Yes, and Alexis has entered her at Madame Guinter's.'

'That German milk-soup kitchen?' Madame Khitrovó referred to the very best private school in Tver. 'Well, Elizabeth, we shall see about it.'

I was present at the conversation—and I should not have been. But since nobody minded me, I stayed where I was. I felt very pleased. Four months of holiday stretched before me. And the talk between Madame Khitrovó and my step-mother had certainly enlarged my knowledge of the new horizons: Madame Khitrovó had no great love for my father.

Yes, I felt pleased. Madame Guinter's establishment would not see me till October. Neither my father nor my step-mother thought about engaging a governess for the months in between, and there was the teasing prospect of a dinner—to be given in my honour! Madame Khitrovó, present at the unpacking of my things, was very angry to see that the pink silk crêpe dress had not even been tacked together. At once it was sent to a leading dressmaker in Tver. Madame Khitrovó and my stepmother between them chose my pink slippers and the first pair of silk stockings I had ever possessed. All those elegant trifles were most unsuitable for my age, and deep down I was conscious of the incongruity. All the same, they gave me great pleasure.

'That dinner, dearest,' said my stepmother, 'is Papa's idea. I think he is very proud of his little daughter. Why, you are not yet twelve—and what a lot you know! The other day I heard you sing something in English—I think.'

Unaccustomed to praise, I blushed wildly. Trained in truthfulness, I said hurriedly:

'I don't know English, Mamma. I learnt a song or two and some short phrases from Nadia's Miss Cottle and that is all. I could not write in English.'

'You are a very modest little girl,' said my stepmother.

Was my father proud of me? I could never tell. Unlike his

second wife and her relations, he was not in the habit of singing our praises. I came to love him deeply in the end but I never lost my awe of him. He seldom if ever caressed us. We saw him at meals and occasionally in the evening. Even little Andrew's tantrums did not make him lose his temper —so even was he with all of us and with the servants. I cannot remember his laughter, but we all treasured his wonderful smile—all the more so because it came seldom enough. He spoke little and always left an impression of having said much. The entire household and all his peasants, as I came to learn later, thought him the kindliest master. His sense of justice was something extraordinary for that generation.

As to my stepmother, he was all the world to her. Always beautiful, she grew lovelier with him in the room. His look made her eyes starry. And even a child was conscious of the deep harmony between them.

As the first days lay behind me, I realized that a certain routine was followed in the house, and most of it was wholly novel to me. We joined the parents at all the meals. The hour of breakfast varied almost from day to day, and my father usually carried his coffee into the library. Young Dunia looked after Andrew at table, but the little boy seemed to eat what he pleased. There were mornings when he refused milk and demanded tea, and my stepmother gave in to him. Emboldened by many such examples, I soon shed the habitual restraint learnt at Trostnikovo—always except in my father's presence. Andrew alone had a more or less regular bedtime, but I sometimes sat in a small corner drawing-room till ten and later, until my father's sudden appearance made me gather up my things and scurry upstairs to my room.

It was a very big household. My stepmother ran it well but it left her fully occupied. Morning conferences with the housekeeper and the chef, flowers, visitors, her own calls, and shopping, made inroads into every day.

So, the first fevered days over, I often found myself alone.

There was the garden to wander about; talks with Masha about our country place I had not yet seen, my toys and books, and, finally, Andrew to cuddle when he was in the humour for it, to play with, and to tell stories to when he felt like listening. A governess would have planned my hours from breakfast till dinner, but my father, having scored a victory about Madame Guinter's school in the autumn, here gave in to his second wife and her relations: 'Little Katia must not be tormented with lessons for a good long time.'

And little Katia was certainly enjoying herself through those first weeks.

The day before that grand dinner, the exquisite pink crêpe dress was brought from the dressmaker's. They spread it out on a sofa for me to see, and I imagined that no princess had ever had so wonderful a frock. The embroidery on the corsage and the full skirt took my breath away. The white silk lining felt good to the touch. There was a rose ribbon for my hair, and when I heard that Masha would curl it into ringlets I felt in the seventh heaven.

The great day came, and Andrew and I were ready. He looked rather adorable in a pale blue silk shirt and black velvet pantaloons. He said to me that I looked passably well. '*Nitchevó sebé*—' which was high praise from a critical younger brother.

When we were summoned downstairs, a fit of shyness swept over me. I let Andrew run on ahead, and paused at the top of the stairs. Was I 'I' or someone else? Through one opened doorway and another I saw rooms crowded with most elegant men and women. They were all my father's guests and all invited because of me! I had a glimpse of a world I had never known and faced an occasion wholly unfamiliar. I have no idea how long I stood there, but at last I saw my stepmother, lovely in pale-rose tulle and a silver-threaded shawl. She sat talking to a fat old lady in purple and beckoned to me.

'Here is Katia, Countess.'

The purple satin beamed on me.

'Goodness, you don't say so! Why it seems only yester-day that I saw her dance the *Rússkaya*, and she was a baby then. My nephew Basil taught her,' she went on, turning to me. 'Katia, do you remember Basil?'

I did—but very vaguely.

'Poor boy.' The purple satin shook her head. 'The brigands killed him in the Caucasus. My dear Katia, how old are you now?'

'Nearly twelve.'

I must say I did not feel very comfortable. The lady talked as though she were an old friend of the family, and I could not remember her at all.

'And Madame Khitrovó has been telling me that you are very clever and speak several languages.'

'Only French and German.'

'Sophie, Sophie,' shouted the purple satin to a younger edition of herself in sky-blue velvet. 'Come here, this is little Katia.'

Such was the beginning. One elegant female after another came up, praised my frock, and marvelled at my 'accomplishments'. My blushes deepened and deepened. I tried to find my stepmother but she was busy with her guests.

At last Philip, the butler, announced dinner, and an alarming number of men came out of the library to take the ladies in. A tall and very handsome gentleman in dark blue tails with gilt buttons offered his arm to my stepmother who gestured to me to come up.

'Monsieur Serbin, may I present my little daughter—a future pupil at Madame Guinter's?'

I dropped a curtsy. The tall man laughed.

'Ah, the queen of the feast, isn't she, and how elegant! Well, young lady,' he went on as we sat down at table, 'I happen to be the head of all the schools in this town—so I am your future commanding officer. And I had better warn you—I am very strict.'

'You don't look it,' I said boldly.

'Don't I?' He held up his napkin and made a face behind it. 'Well, now, how many languages do you know?'

'Two and a half.'

'Which half?'

'English.'

'Ah—and what about history? Who was the first to cross the Alps?'

'Fancy starting an examination at dinner!' exclaimed his other neighbour, a rather mature young lady in a dress of deep pink. 'I am sure our dear Katia is sick to death of all those grammars and things.'

I did not even know her name, but she smiled at me, and the last shreds of bewilderment left me. I felt I was indeed queen of the feast. I looked up and down the enormous table, which stretched the entire length of the ballroom, and said to myself that all the flowers, fruit and gold and silver plate were set out in my honour. My stepmother, however busy in giving orders to footmen and looking after the guests, still found time for a glance and a smile in my direction. So did my father from the other end of the table, and now one guest, now another, turned to me with some flattering remark about my frock.

Came the roast and the champagne, and my father got up, glass in hand.

'To our dear Katia—'

That I had never expected, and my cheeks turned as scarlet as two peonies in full bloom. At a sign from my stepmother, I left my place and made for the head of the table to thank my father. As I was turning away from him, a young footman, laden with a tray of gravy-boats, stumbled against me so violently that one of the gravy-boats overturned.

The front of my dress almost soaked in the gravy and the flounced hem spattered all over were proof enough that my finery was irrevocably ruined. One after another, the ladies present began recommending ice, salt, dry flannel, but it was obvious that the rose crêpe and white silk were stained for good. I was sent to change upstairs, and returned, wearing a modest white muslin, to find everybody having coffee.

'Ah, young lady,' exclaimed Monsieur Serbin, 'now that is much better.'

'Indeed,' chimed in the purple satin, 'I, too, think that white suits Katia far better than pink.'

'*Enfin, la voilà mise en enfant,*' ejaculated an elderly cousin of my stepmother's, a golden lorgnon to her eyes, and at once I remembered that the elderly cousin had been most extravagant in her praises of my finery.

I sat down in a corner. After the first few remarks nobody took much notice of me. They had had a good dinner, had enjoyed themselves and lavished reckless compliments on a little girl in a pink crêpe frock far too elegant for her age. But now the dinner was over, they began thinking about their carriages, and the very brief reign of the queen of the feast had come to its close. Some of them had a kiss to spare for a girl in plain white muslin—but not all. The pink dress had been important, not its wearer. I was glad when that day came to an end.

I do not remember any more parties of that kind. My stepmother had told me it was all my father's wish and she may well have thought so, but somehow I was left with the impression that Madame Khitrovó had been really responsible for an occasion which, having started by puffing up my vanity to an absurd extent, ended by wounding it very deeply. Not till much later did I learn how salutary that wound had been.

Meanwhile, holidays continued. Little by little Nicholas shed his remoteness and busied himself in entertaining his sister. Fireworks, a dolls' theatre, treasure-hunts in the garden, *tableaux-vivants* succeeded one another. Whenever our parents were out—and that happened often enough—

even little Andrew was allowed to stay up much later than his usual bedtime.

On one occasion when my stepmother came back alone from a big public dinner, she found me sitting on the stairs, hair dishevelled, frock all crumpled, and one stocking down to my ankle, my right hand pulling at a piece of toffee which was held by Andrew, and neither of us could pull really hard because we were laughing so much.

'Dears, dears,' she scolded gently, 'you should have been in bed hours ago, Andrew. Now what have you been up to?'

'We had a dolls' supper, Mamma.'

'I was the cook,' announced Andrew, forgetting the toffee for a moment. 'I gave them raisins and plums and chocolate—all together with rice. I cooked in the nursery, Mamma,' he added.

'And Andrew's tin soldiers were paired with my dolls.'

'Vania got us some ice, too, and we had a cranberry cordial.'

'And music—'

'And my tin soldiers danced, Mamma.'

'It was such fun, and Nicholas thought of it all.'

'Well, Katia,' my stepmother said to me the next day, 'I am so glad you are not bored here.'

'Bored? Mamma, I am in paradise.'

And so it continued for the first month, and then . . . First of all, with two young maids to wait on me, I got more and more untidy. I no longer folded my clothes at night but just threw them about on the floor for Dunia or Masha to put them away. My toys and dolls remained uncared for. When Nicholas was busy, I took to wandering about from the garden into the gallery and back again. I teased the canaries, teased the cat, teased the cook's dog. My books were all on the shelves in my room—but I never looked at them. And at last came the first of my many quarrels with poor little Andrew.

He was still very much of a baby for his seven years, but

143

he was a very independent little fellow. A priest's widow used to come in the mornings to teach him, and the rest of the day he spent very much as he pleased—but he always knew how to amuse himself, and he would spend hours colouring some picture or other, or contriving some fantastic shape, its meaning clear to himself alone, out of odd pieces of cardboard. Once he asked me for the loan of my box of colours, and I refused. By way of a reprisal Andrew pulled so hard at my pinafore that a part of the hem came off.

'You are nasty and rude,' I shouted at him, when Masha came in to tell us that the priest's widow was waiting for Andrew. He had his lessons in a little room behind the hall, and I knew he would be out of the way for a good hour or so. And what did I decide to do 'to pay him out' for that miserable pinafore which, anyhow, would have been speedily mended by one of the maids?

In the day-nursery, between the stove and one of the windows, Andrew kept his cavalry—a collection of some fifteen or twenty toy horses. I ran upstairs, pulled out all their tails, tied them together, tore into the garden and threw them into the heart of thick bushes at the very end.

Our parents were away for the day. Nicholas was at home. Presently, as I sat in my room, I heard Andrew yelling the house down. I did not move. Then the door opened. It was Nicholas, and I hardly recognized him, so cold were his eyes.

'Did you pull those tails out?' he asked, his voice icy.

I nodded.

'Why?'

'He was rude. He tore my pinafore.'

'You are five years older than Andrew. Don't you see that you and I together must take care of him? Our mother is dead.'

'What are you talking about? Mamma spoils Andrew like anything.'

'Yes,' Nicholas said, 'she may well do so now—but she

may have other children in the future, and Andrew is her stepson.' He added abruptly: 'Where did you put them—I mean the horses' tails?'

I told him, and he sent one of the gardeners to find them. By tea-time they were all in place again, gummed in by Nicholas, and on seeing me come into the nursery, Andrew ran up to me:

'Look, look, Katia darling, all my horses have recovered.'

I sat by him and I kissed him. He had forgotten all about the pinafore, and I was not brave enough to acknowledge my own trespass. Nicholas was mending a tiny saddle of one of the horses. I spoke to him, and he answered rather curtly. For some days after his manner to me remained cold.

## 15 *That very idle interlude*

Our garden at Tver was enormous. None the less, it was a town garden, and by the time June drew to its close, all the trees and shrubs looked dusty and clouds of thin grey-yellow dust spiralled from under our feet whenever we ran down a path. We all longed for the country, and I had hoped that we would go straight down to Zvietkovo, my father's place about thirty miles distant. But he was having some alterations and additions made to the house and all the farm buildings were being repaired. On top of that my step-mother received a letter from Madame Khitrovó to say that she expected us at Dubky the first day of July and would not accept any excuses. 'And I shall be offended if you stay less than three weeks,' my stepmother read aloud. My father said nothing.

'What do I say, Alexis?' she asked almost timidly.

'Tell your mother we shall be there on the first of July,' he replied and left the room, and both my brothers ran after him.

Having never seen Dubky, I was wildly curious about it. Some instinct told me not to ask questions of my step-mother. I found Nicholas and Andrew busily carving a boat under the shade of an old lime at the very bottom of the garden.

'It is dreadful, Katia,' announced Andrew. 'You won't like it at all. The rooms are so dark and you are not allowed to run up and down the stairs. They never open the windows and are always afraid of the rain,' he added contemptuously.

'The park is good,' said Nicholas, 'when we can get into

it. They are always at you—what are you going to do and where are you going?'

'What do they do all day long?' I wanted to know.

'They sit and they talk. They sit and they eat,' Nicholas said gloomily. 'One of the drawing-rooms is called the bosky room—its walls are painted all over with trees. That, I suppose, is enough for them—they hardly ever go out. You wait till we get to Zvietkovo, Katia—we spend whole days out of doors—wet or fine—it doesn't matter. At Dubky they expect you to change your shoes every time you go in or out.'

'Yes, but there are ponies and puppies,' offered Andrew.

'Ah, but can we get to the stables when we want to?'

The prospect certainly did not please any of us. I tried to cheer them up by saying it was only for three weeks.

'And I have to be back in college by the middle of August,' retorted Nicholas. 'So that means just a month at Zvietkovo, and I don't come home again till Christmas!'

I thought hard.

'Couldn't all of us get really ill before the first of July?'

But, unfortunately, none of us knew how to set about getting really ill. Andrew tried valiantly by getting all his clothes soaked in the garden the day one terrific shower came on the heels of another, but the boy was so sturdy that he did not even get an ordinary cold.

I believe my stepmother knew all about our dislike of Dubky, but I remember clearly that none of us discussed it when she was present. Not even Andrew gave a single airing to his many grievances.

Dubky lay about twenty-five miles from Tver. The road led through a deep forest of elm and birch. My stepmother, Nicholas, Andrew and I got out of the carriage to ease the horses after a fairly steep hill. The midday heat had gone. It felt cool, and the air was fragrant with fresh mown hay and wood strawberries. Wild duck flew overhead and from the heart of the wood came the echo of a song. I looked about

147

and clapped my hands.

'Mamma, isn't it lovely here? So very peaceful—just trees and trees! Couldn't we build a hut and settle down here?'

My stepmother did not laugh at my enthusiasm. She merely said:

'For one thing, my love, the wood does not belong to us. For another, I know there are many marshy spots in it and lots of frogs, and you are afraid of them. Finally, this is the high road from Tver—there may well be drunks and all kind of undesirable folk ... You would never sleep in peace in your hut.'

I blushed.

'It was just an idea, Mamma.'

'I know,' she nodded, 'some ideas are good to play with.'

The wood and the hill were the only remarkable features of the landscape surrounding Dubky. Flat fields of pasture and arable, with an occasional coppice of undergrown oaks and stunted firs, led us to the village. The green roof of an ugly timbered church caught the westering sun as we drove through the imposing wrought iron gates. The long avenue was flat and straight as an arrow, and I had ample time to look at a great sprawling house, its red roof, its colonnaded porch, and its beautifully shaped windows. As the carriage drew nearer, I saw that all the windows were closed.

I remember smelling leather and incense in the dim hall and clutching my stepmother's hand, so afraid was I of being lost in those unfamiliar shadows. She led me into a drawing-room—not so dim but absolutely airless. And there was Madame Khitrovó, her soldier son on leave from the Caucasus, his lovely but languid wife, and her two nieces, who, I had already been told, would be 'my closest companions' at Dubky.

The tumult of the first greetings was over at last. Madame Khitrovó and her daugther-in-law vying with each other in their welcome. Within five minutes I received so much praise that I felt as though I had grown several inches since leaving

Tver.

Tea, to my great relief, was served on the balcony at the back of the house. At table, I had a good look at my future 'closest companions'. The elder, Larissa, about three years older than I, was pale, wore a white gown much too elegant for her age, had very little conversation, and pecked at her food. The younger, Julie, a plump red-cheeked body of fourteen, dressed in an unbecoming yellow muslin, was obviously a chatterbox who had very little of interest to say.

Nicholas had already warned me about the meals at Dubky. 'They are interminable.' Now tea had been drunk and food eaten—but Madame Khitrovó still sat in her huge armchair at the head of the table. The garden was there—and beyond it lay the park. I have no idea how long we would have been on the balcony if Andrew had not raised his shrill voice:

'Katia has not seen the garden yet—'

Permission was given, together with the warning not to stay out too long and to keep away from the kitchen-gardens. Larissa stayed behind, but Julie waddled down the steps and followed us. She chattered all the time and my brothers did not listen. They had met Julie before and knew what to expect. But in common courtesy I felt that I must listen.

On that first day I learned quite a lot about the inhabitants of Dubky. One had to watch one's step with Madame Khit-rovó, lisped Julie. 'Aunt Nina and Uncle Dimitry are very strict but kind. Aunt Natalie is an angel. I think Larissa is very jealous of you. Aunt Natalie says you know seven languages. Larissa thinks it is "interesting" to look pale—so she eats hardly anything. And I am a greedy... Are you afraid of bats? There are lots at Dubky. Have you been to Georgia? Uncle Dimitry's regiment is there. Have you read any novels? Larissa keeps French novels under her mattress. She knows I won't tell. She is so clever, but I don't mind— I am pretty. Do you believe in witches?' She lisped on and on, peppering me with questions and never waiting for answers. 'An officer in Georgia saw a real witch—'

'Flying on a broomstick or on a poker?' asked Nicholas suddenly, his irony obvious even to Julie. She pouted, announced that she was tired, and turned back to the house.

We had been told not to go near the kitchen-gardens. But the main garden at Dubky was more or less a glorified kitchen-garden. Rows of cabbage and onions alternated with overgrown rose bushes and clumps of peonies. Stocks, sunflowers and larkspurs grew in wild abundance—with great swathes of love-in-the-mist neighbouring raspberry canes and strawberry beds. Space and colour were certainly there— but I felt it was no garden to make a friend of. There were no trees and no surprising, exciting corners. We reached the edge of the park—separated by a straggling honeysuckle hedge. Beyond lay an apparent immensity—all dark green shot through here and there by the brilliant gold of the dying sun. My brothers gestured right and left, pointing at the landmarks they knew—a clump of old beeches, a fir, two elms 'good for climbing' and—far away—the reddened silver of a big pond.

But there was no time to explore the park. We turned back to the house. The tea-table had been cleared away, but the grown-ups were still on the balcony. My father sat on the topmost step, a cigar between his teeth. Madame Khitrovó and my stepmother were not there, but the two aunts, a few visitors staying in the house, and Larissa and Julie were all there. My stepmother's brother was holding forth about an ambush made by the Circassians in the mountains near Piatigorsk where, had it not been for the bravery of General Ermolov and another officer, two Russian battalions would have been put to the sword. I made my way to a stool in the farthest corner of the balcony. It was soon obvious to me that everybody present had already had their fill of the stories about the Caucasian heroes. In my turn I closed my eyes and was asleep.

'Supper is served.' The butler's sonorous voice woke me, and I opened my eyes to the summer dark.

We made our way to a long dining-room dimly lit by wax candles stood here and there in silver-gilt sticks. The meal started with enormous bowls of *bortch*. When it came to a stuffed turkey, smothered in various garnishes, neither Nicholas nor I could manage it. Madame Khitrovó allowed us to go to bed. Preceded by a footman with a candle, we passed from one big low-ceilinged room into another. All the windows were shuttered 'because of the bats', explained the man, and the scent of mint, strawberries, incense and lampade oil lingered everywhere.

In my room a sleepy country girl waited for me. She seemed greatly surprised at my request to bring me water for washing. She fetched a huge copper jug quickly enough and gasped when I said I did not need her any more.

'I always manage on my own. Please, what is your name?'

'Seraphima, Miss—but what about helping you with your shoes?'

For all answer I took off my shoes and pulled off my stockings.

'What foreign ways, Miss!' marvelled Seraphima. She smothered a yawn and left me.

I should have asked her about the shutters. Their bars and bolts were so intricate that—wrestle with them as I might, I could not budge them. I said my prayers and leapt into bed but, accustomed to fresh air in my room, I could not sleep.

Presently through the thin wooden wall I heard Madame Khitrovó's deep voice giving last-minute instructions to her maid. There was something to tell the cook about an egg pie and chickens. A cow had gone lame—'tell Timothy'. Three dozen wax candles to be bought for some feast or other . . . Listening, I grew drowsy. 'Father Foma . . . Cherries are ripe . . . time to pickle them . . . Another cow gone lame? Tell Stepan I must see him tomorrow . . . less Three oaks to come down . . . Not enough barley sown . . . Father Foma . . .

No, geese would be better... Saffron should be ordered...
Don't forget... The cherries...'

At last I fell into a broken sleep and woke up with a splitting headache.

'Night-air?' echoed Madame Khitrovó after everybody had remarked on my pallor at breakfast. 'Whoever heard of people sleeping with their windows open?'

None the less, Seraphima had her orders, and my shutters were neither bolted nor barred that evening. I opened the windows wide, snuffed out the candle, and never gave a single thought to bats.

My three weeks at Dubky gave me much room for thought.

Madame Khitrovó, born in St. Petersburg and having spent all her married life in Moscow, was now wholly a countrywoman and very much of a matriarch. Widowed in 1831, she had retired to Dubky, left to her in her father's will, and managed the vast estate entirely on her own. The big house in Tver, where we now lived, together with a much smaller place than Dubky, formed part of my step-mother's marriage settlement.

Madame Khitrovó kept an open house. Every day visitors who chanced to call in the morning were invariably urged to stay to luncheon, to dinner, to supper. Every day was most rigidly punctuated by meals: breakfast, luncheon, dinner, tea, supper, evening tea. Men guests spent their leisure in fishing, cards and endless discussions of land problems. The ladies were engrossed in embroidery, tatting, a little singing and music, and interminable talks about funerals, weddings, latest provincial scandals, larder and still-room. On rare occasions Madame Khitrovó and her daughter Natalie went to do shopping at Tver. The annual excursion to Moscow yielded food for discussion for weeks before and after. The post came twice a week. Neither books nor periodicals nor yet newspapers came to Dubky. The great mahogany book-cases in one of the drawing-rooms were filled with porcelain.

The only book I remember seeing there was a Psalter of Madame Khitrovó's. Larissa's French novels must have been smuggled in most cleverly—I never saw one of them.

Not till many years later did I realize that the kind of life led at Dubky was followed on innumerable manors up and down the Russian Empire. It was a little self-contained world. Wines, sugar and spices were the only commodities bought for the table. Everything else was home-grown and home-made. Madame Khitrovó did not even have to order wheels for the farm carts. Certain implements had to be purchased—such as spades and scythes, but their repairs were carried out at home. Apart from such matters, all interests remained strictly provincial: the Governor-General's receptions at Tver, the few balls given there during the year, the amazing story of a nobleman's widow appearing at a merchant's wedding, and a year-old fashion brought either from St. Petersburg or Moscow. The Caucasus was on the map because Madame Khitrovó's son served there, and Poland remained an accursed country because her husband had been killed in the 1831 mutiny. Otherwise the world did not exist.

And how desperately bored I was with it all! My 'closest companions' did not help in the least. Larissa hardly ever appeared except at meals, when she had nothing to say. Julie never stopped talking about nothing, and within a few days I began avoiding her. The first day's headache served me most unkindly: Madame Khitrovó decided that long excursions were bad for me and I must needs stay indoors when my two brothers enjoyed themselves as best they could in the stable-yard and in the park.

On top of it all, everybody did their best to turn me into a prodigy. Most unfortunately, my parents would leave Dubky in the morning and not get back till after supper: my father was carrying out several alterations at Zvietkovo, his place about ten miles distant, and he felt that his presence alone would speed up the work. My stepmother, naturally, went

with him. I had a feeling even thus early that my father did
not care for Dubky in the least.

I would be introduced to every caller in some such way:
'That is my Alexis's daughter. You have no idea how
clever she is. Plays the piano, dances, reads and writes in four
languages. Brought up in a foreign way by a cousin, but I
must say it did not do her much harm. Why, the child is
not twelve yet and knows such a lot, and what a memory!'

The first time such a preamble made me blush and squirm
with embarrassment. Towards the end of my stay at Dubky
I was taking it all for granted. Natalie Khitrovó never tired
of making me recite poetry in the drawing-room. Her sister-
in-law showered almost daily presents on me. Any foolish-
ness I might have uttered at table was repeated on all sides.
'How witty is our Katia!'

I was not, but I felt pleased at such remarks. And yet,
perversely, I was very unhappy at Dubky. For one thing, on
occasions I would be present at conversations I should never
have heard. It was for Madame Khitrovó to send me out of
the room. She did not, and my poor stepmother would
never have dared to give a single order—even to me—in her
own mother's presence. I remember one morning with my
father already gone to Zvietkovo and my stepmother remaining behind because of some very old friends coming
to dinner. It was raining hard and we were in the bosky
room, Madame Khitrovó, my stepmother and I. There had
been a somewhat prolonged discussion of a solemn Te Deum
to be sung later on in the week because of some minor feast.
My stepmother said rather carefully:

'I am so sorry, Mamma, but Alexis and I have to be at
Tver that day.'

Madame Khitrovó dropped her needle.

'But it is a feast-day, Elizabeth.'

My stepmother said nothing and bent her lovely head over
the needlework in her lap.

'Yes, yes,' said Madame Khitrovó angrily. 'It is always

the same now. I might not exist for you ... It is always your husband and his children. Why, you have left off all the old ways—married to a foreigner that you are.'

'Mamma, Alexis is not a foreigner. He belongs to the Orthodox Church.'

'He may do, but who but a foreigner would have sent his daughter away?' demanded Madame Khitrovó. 'Did you not tell me that Katia said her prayers in three languages! Gracious heavens, I trust my own French is as fluent as my Russian, but I would never dream of addressing my Maker in a foreign tongue! And Katia herself told me that they were hardly ever taken to church at Trostnikovo! I ask you!'

My stepmother murmured:

'All of it is changed, Mamma. She goes every Sunday, and we keep the fasts.'

'But the harm was done,' insisted Madame Khitrovó. 'And there you are—going to do some business or other on a feast-day. What will Father Foma think, I ask you?'

That very day Madame Khitrovó had given me an exquisite porcelain doll's tea-set. At that moment I almost wished I had the courage to run, fetch the present, and smash it to pieces at her feet. I felt that she was unkind, stupid and muddling. Her jeers at my 'foreign' upbringing certainly did not correspond with her fervour at 'showing me off' and her tireless eulogies of my 'accomplishments'. At the very first opportunity I slipped out of the bosky room and ran upstairs to indulge in a bout of weeping. I was so sorry for my stepmother.

Madame Khitrovó lacked logic in more senses than one. She had told me on arrival that I would be my own mistress so long as I stayed under her roof—but within the very first hours I realized that my life was hedged about with most bewildering taboos. I was forbidden the kitchen-gardens for a reason never explained to me. The poultry-yard and the stables were also out of bounds 'because of the dirt'. The park was too far away—'you might get another headache'.

The evening before we left, I happened to be in my room and leant out of the window. From a corner I could not see, I heard my father's voice:

'Elizabeth, if Katia does not mend her manners when we get home, I shall send her away before the autumn. I hear that today at luncheon she again made most unkindly fun of Andrew, and your sister-in-law thought it was so clever.'

'Yes, Nina told me about it. But, Alexis, Katia did not mean any harm. It is true that Andrew is a little greedy, and Katia did not make fun of him—she merely said that a cherry-tree would grow in his tummy if he had another helping of the cherry-tart.'

'She is always either poking fun at poor Andrew, or scaring him,' said my father.

I know I should never have eavesdropped. I tiptoed away from the window, my ears burning. That evening I hated everybody at Dubky—including myself.

# 16 *'Papa, it is heavenly . . .'*

To this day there steals a warmth into my heart when I remember Zvietkovo and the first months we spent there. It was neither house nor grounds, however pleasant and spacious, but something so radiant, satisfying, something that lent pleasure to the most prosaic daily task. Compared with Trostnikovo and Dubky, Zvietkovo seemed a humble enough manor. True that it had two villages, several fields, a river and a great wood of silver birch and elm, but it had no park, no magnificent lakes and waterfalls. Its few hot-houses did not stretch into misty distances—the way they did at Trostnikovo, its stabling provided enough space for about ten horses, and the house was a house, not a mansion in the grand Rastrelli style. In its ballroom about fifteen couples could stand up—and no more. It had only one spacious drawing-room. The three others were small and cosy. Instead of a great library there was a room my father used as his study. There were two balconies, but the porch was not colonnaded. With her unerring taste, my stepmother did not crowd the rooms with furniture upholstered in velvet and brocade. She had, as I learnt, ordered the chintzes from England. They were gay, appropriate and unusual for that part of the country.

The drive was rather short, bordered by old oaks, and the candid face of the house stood in full view as soon as you came to the gates. The main road to Tver ran past. The hateful Dubky lay about ten miles to the south-west.

When I was brought to Zvietkovo that August day in 1841, I saw it all for the very first time.

The estate had belonged to my Uncle Adalbert. Not till old Agatha's visit to Trostnikovo had I heard about his existence. Now, back with my own family, I knew very little more. My brothers knew no more than I did. My stepmother was rather evasive, and I stood in such awe of my father that any probing would have been out of the question. He never mentioned his brother at all.

My Uncle Adalbert had lived and died at Zvietkovo, but he could not have been buried there since I never found his grave either in the church or in the graveyard. He had lived all by himself in a great eighteenth-century house. My stepmother explained that it had been pulled down and a new one built. 'Your father did not think the old house would be convenient,' was all she said. Zvietkovo being entailed, it passed to my father automatically on his brother's death.

Only years and years later, when I had done with all manner of schooling and returned to Zvietkovo, a fully fledged débutante, did my stepmother tell me the story, having first warned me never to mention it to my father.

The story was most fantastic, and I cannot now remember how my stepmother had come to hear of it in the first place —most likely from someone in the neighbourhood.

'Your uncle,' said my stepmother, 'lived and died a Roman Catholic. As a young man, he had travelled much abroad. On his return to Zvietkovo, he began leading the life of a recluse. There were a few servants in the house, and they were all foreigners, and I suppose that did not increase his popularity. The story went that during his foreign travels he had fallen in love with a woman on a portrait and bought it for a very high price—it must have been the work of some great master long, long time ago. He brought it with him to Zvietkovo and began dabbling in magic so as to bring the portrait to life. It used to be whispered in the neighbourhood that he had succeeded—but, of course, that was nonsense.'

158

'Did he quarrel with my father?' I then asked.

'I never heard of any quarrel. Your uncle just kept himself to himself. It was all rather sad. He was much older than your father. Zvietkovo was given to him by the Empress Catherine. Your father, naturally, had heard all those stories, and it was wise of him to have the old house pulled down when he came into the estate.' And my stepmother added: 'I should say your uncle must have been a very unhappy man. He had no friends. His great fortune did not seem to give him any pleasure. He came to Russia as a boy and he lived and died a foreigner—even though he was a Russian subject like your father. I did hear a rumour that in his magical studies he would be helped by an uncle of his either in Vienna or Augsburg, but I don't really know. I did hear that he was very obstinate and used his title to the very end. Your father would not dream of doing so. Your family was given the patent of untitled hereditary nobility by the Empress Catherine—so it was wrong of your uncle to go on using that foreign title.'

But in 1841 I knew none of it, and somehow I do not believe that my Uncle Adalbert could have been a very unhappy man: Zvietkovo was far too pleasant and cheerful a place.

There were two shrubberies of oak and beech on either side of the drive. The garden started at the back of the house, an enchanting pleasance with paths curving this way and that, rich in lilac, laburnum, honeysuckle and bear-berry bushes. It was big enough to lose one's self in, but not too big for intimate and detailed knowledge. There was a small pond girdled by old weeping-willows, and several clumps of old limes at the end of a path where a wicket gate led to the orchard, the kitchen-garden, and a lovely wilderness of tree and shrub—all apparently self-sown. The poultry-yard, the farm and the stables lay to the left of the garden. To the right, one field after another ran into a deep lilac distance where the great woods began.

There was nothing remarkable; nothing to make important people from St. Petersburg or Moscow come, make sketches, or write a book. The Province of Tver was enormous and Zvietkovo was but one dot on that map.

But what a beloved dot! As soon as I jumped out of the carriage, I ran, rounded the house, and found myself in the garden. I remember I stood still for a few moments. Then I clapped my hands. My brothers ran up to join me. Together we spent that heavenly August morning in marking one corner after another until a footman ran us to earth at the end of the orchard. What an effort it was to turn indoors and sit down to dinner! My stepmother looked at our flushed faces and said to my father:

'My friend, they are at home here already.'

He replied by one of his very rare smiles.

We certainly were at home—much more so than in the big house in Tver. Zvietkovo was entailed, and that very summer Nicholas began his initiation into the numberless mysteries of estate business. He listened to bailiffs' reports in the tiny wooden shed which served as estate office. Nearly every morning after breakfast, my father and he would ride away into the fields and the woods. Andrew and I were left alone, and we followed our stepmother all over the place, into the housekeeper's room, into the larder, into the garden to look at the newly made beds of roses and peonies. If she had any business in the orchard or the poultry-yard, we were always there. And she did not mind any of it. She laughed at the inane remarks we might make to the cowman, at the absurd directions we gave to the gardener about the strawberry beds. In her sun bonnet and a white print dress, my stepmother looked far younger than she did at Dubky or even at Tver. When her morning tasks were over, she took us to her own sitting-room, where we drank milk and nibbled sponge-cakes. In those first weeks at Zvietkovo my stepmother was more or less an elder sister. She never scolded; she never gave orders. She smiled, she coaxed, and won us wholly.

All was peace between Andrew and myself.

Except for one absurd interlude.

We had not been at Zvietkovo for a fortnight when Madame Khitrovó sent a peremptory *ukaz* for us to come and dine the following day to say good-bye to her son and his wife who were leaving for the Caucasus. My father at once said that he would be busy most of the day with a timber merchant from Bologoye. But we three could find no such excuses. Much to my displeasure Masha starched and ironed my white muslin.

'Never mind, *báryshna*,' she comforted me when she was doing my hair. 'I heard the mistress say to Philip that you would be back for tea. The time will pass quickly.'

It was a dreadfully hot day. It proved a dreadfully long dinner. At last, we came out on the balcony. Pale Larissa was as taciturn as ever. Plump, pink Julie, in green muslin which did not suit her at all, confided in me that she hated the very idea of going back to the Caucasus. I said I was sorry. She began telling me about the new gowns she was taking. I stopped listening and looked about. My two brothers, as I guessed, must have slipped off to the stables. Madame Khitrovó, her son and his wife were not there. Julie and I were sitting on the lowest step of the balcony. I could see my stepmother in an armchair at the opposite end of the balcony. The only guest remaining, a retired hussar colonel with a thin swarthy face and very long moustaches, sat by her side, talking to her.

To my great pleasure, Julie remembered something about her packing and left me. I turned my head, waiting for the first opportunity to run up the steps and ask my stepmother if it was time to have our carriage brought to the porch. But the tiresome, garrulous hussar was still at it. And suddenly I heard him say:

'By the way, we are still astonished that anyone as young and pretty as yourself should have married M. Almedingen. Why, it is just as though you have become head of an orphanage—'

My stepmother at once rose to her feet. Never before or after had I seen her so angry. Her eyes were almost black. Her voice rang icy:

'Colonel, I have known you since I was a child, but that does not give you the right to insult me. I am one of the happiest women in the country, and how dare you call my family an orphanage?'

And she turned her back on him. She had not seen me. I wanted to run up the steps of the balcony and to scratch the man's eyes out. I prayed that his horses would bolt on his way home . . .

Yet I sat very still until my brothers ran up to tell me that it was time to say good-bye to everybody.

'What is the matter, Katia?' my stepmother asked when we were in the carriage. 'You look as though everything has disagreed with you.'

'It is the heat, Mamma, and oh, I thought that dinner would never end . . .' and, all caution forgotten, I burst out, 'Please never take me to Dubky again. I hate it . . .'

She gave me a peculiar glance but said nothing.

My sullenness had not gone by the time we were home. I did not like telling my stepmother that I had heard the hussar's impertinent words. I could not get rid of an unpleasant, disturbing sediment and, all unwittingly, poor Andrew furnished me with a chance to vent my bad humour on him.

We were just finishing tea when he asked suddenly:

'Papa, would a million roubles take up a lot of room, do you think?'

'What a very odd question!' replied my father. 'What makes you ask it?'

'Well, Katia said this morning that her Cousin Nicholas at Trostnikovo had a million. I should say he must have lots and lots of trunks to keep all that money in.'

My father glanced at me rather ironically.

162

'You had better ask your sister, Andrew. She may have seen those trunks.'

'I have never said anything about any trunks,' I broke in heatedly. 'I merely said that Uncle Nicholas was very wealthy, and that is true.'

But Andrew would not let me off.

'No, no, Katia,' he cried, 'you did talk of a million—why, this very morning when we were all walking in the oak coppice, and I said that nobody except the Tsar could have so much money, and you laughed and said that it was rubbish and that a neighbour of theirs had even more money. You did! You did!'

I turned on him angrily:

'Stop making up such stories, Andrew. I never said anything of the kind.'

'It is not a story,' yelled Andrew. 'You did—you did—'

'Nicholas,' my father broke in, 'you were there. Did your sister mention a million?'

'Yes, Papa, she said she thought the Mirkovs had about a million, but she never mentioned any trunks.'

'There you are!' I glared at Andrew. 'You and your trunks! Always inventing things, you little liar, you—' and I would have gone on if he had not burst out crying and my stepmother had not said severely:

'Stop at once, Katia! What a shame—Andrew is much younger than you—'

'And you please tell Andrew to stop lying,' I retorted rudely and was at once sent into my room.

There, the hussar's impertinent allusion to 'the orphanage', Nicholas's warning that our stepmother might well have other children, old Agatha's dark hints about a difficult future, together with my stepmother upholding Andrew in the day's stupid quarrel, all of it rushed into my mind, and I gave free vent to most disgusting self-pity.

'Not wanted anywhere... Just an orphan... What Nadia used to say long ago... It is all true... And Mamma does prefer Andrew to me... Shall I ever be wanted anywhere?'

My handkerchief was a soaked rag. I forgot that I had no pinafore on that day, and took to rubbing my face with the clean white muslin skirt, but my tears ran on and on. It was in such a condition that my stepmother found me on coming into my room about an hour later. She did not send for Masha or Tania. She made me change my ruined white muslin, wash my face and tidy my hair. Then she sat down and looked at me hard.

'Are you the Katia I took to my heart three months ago?' she asked. 'Peevish, sullen, bad-tempered... I simply can't believe you could have changed so... And what have you done today? I had so hoped you would live peaceably with Andrew here at Zvietkovo. Now your father says you are to go as a full boarder to Madame Guinter's, and I can't argue with him. I had so hoped to keep you at home till next August when you go to Moscow.'

I sat on the floor, my eyes bent, for some minutes, and then I burst out:

'Mamma, if you had other children, would you care less for us?'

Her lovely face looked at once sad and astonished.

'Who has been talking to you?' she wanted to know.

'Well,' I mumbled, determined not to give Nicholas away, 'you had little Varia.'

'My poor child, my dearest,' she said very softly. 'You should have come to me as soon as that idea got into your mind.'

Quietly, her eyes on my face, she went on to explain that she had had a very difficult time with little Varia and that later the doctors told my father she could never have another child. I listened greedily.

'So Nicholas, Andrew and I are not really orphans?'

Her cheeks went pink.

'My poor darling, you should not have given another

thought to that old man's words. I am only sorry you should have heard them. Now come down and make your peace with Andrew.'

I hesitated.

'Do you know that boy has a heart of gold? Whenever you have a headache, he will keep quiet for hours in the nursery for fear that the least noise might disturb you.'

I found Andrew engaged in trying to make a small basket. He was not particularly good at it. He puffed and panted.

'Nicholas might finish it,' he said at last. 'It is for you, Katia. Tania said she had broken the little box where you kept your ribbons. I thought a basket might do.'

We had a most happy time over supper that evening.

My father's decision about Madame Guinter's held firm. The very day after Nicholas's departure, my stepmother told me to take all my books into a small room at the back of the house.

'Put in about a couple of hours' work this morning. Papa will be so pleased when he gets home from Tver tonight.'

I looked at the tattered textbooks which I had not opened for several months—Bogdanov's *Catechism*, Ishimova's *Russian History*, someone's manual of geography, some three or four exercise-books filled with translations corrected by Cousin Sophie and Mademoiselle Berg and, finally, my favourite German anthology. I opened the latter. *'Es war einmal ein armer Knabe* . . .' I began that very short tale three times over, conscious that the meaning of the simplest words kept escaping me. I tried to conjugate *avoir* and realized that I had forgotten the present participle. I opened the geography book and found the world map at the end— with not a single place-name on it. What was the name of the great river in the heart of South America? I had forgotten. My inky hands were shaking when I picked up the *Russian History*. I used to know practically every page of Ishimova's excellent book. Now I opened it at the chapter

165

about Tsar Michael, covered the page with my hand, and tried to remember the name of his predecessor.

'A prodigy?' I thought bitterly. 'I have forgotten everything except a handful of poems.'

It was the twentieth of August. October the tenth was the day fixed for my going to Madame Guinter's—to be laughed at by girls younger than myself . . .

'They shan't,' I said angrily to myself. 'I am going to work hard,' and I seized the geography book once again.

But the months of unpardonable idleness were taking their toll. The very effort of concentrating on South American rivers made me drowsy. In the end I fell fast asleep. My stepmother woke me up just before luncheon.

'I think your father is right, dearest,' she said calmly.

Within a week we were back at Tver. Madame Khitrovó, coming to dine and to spend the night, argued that it was wrong to allow me 'to sit over those dreadful books' for hours and hours, but she did not say so in my father's presence, and my stepmother received all those arguments in silence.

It was in the early days of October that I reaped a rare reward. My father came into my room, sat down at the table, picked up now one book, now another, and shot questions at me. Wholly taken aback by this improvised examination, I blushed, stammered and stumbled at first. Then my voice got steadier and steadier. The answers came out one by one. At last, my father laid down the book and smiled at me.

'I don't think I am going to be ashamed of my daughter at Madame Guinter's. You have certainly been working hard these last five weeks, Katia. I am so glad,' and, getting up, he stooped and gave me one of his very rare kisses.

The caress emboldened me.

'Papa, it is heavenly.'

'What is?'

'Zvietkovo—and my books,' I told him.

166

## 17 *Off to school*

Madame Khitrovó was furious when she heard that I was going to Madame Guinter's as a full boarder. She said it made no sense since all the girls living at Tver were day-pupils. She said she was sure I would be starved there because 'the Germans understood nothing about food'. She said she was pretty certain that life in that house would be like penal servitude, with lessons from early morning till late at night. She said that Madame Guinter's was no suitable *pensionnat* for a nobleman's daughter because some of the pupils belonged to the merchant class. She said a great many other things and succeeded in upsetting my stepmother, but my father would not change his mind.

And, though I heard everything said by Madame Khitrovó, I was glad that my father stood firm.

I had not the slightest idea of what life in a boarding-school would be like and my feelings were necessarily mixed, but I still remember looking forward to that day in October. It seemed at once an adventure and an opportunity. More-over, Nicholas had gone to his military college, Andrew's mornings were occupied by his tutor, my stepmother was busy, and I needed companionship. It was, of course, good to realize that I would be coming home every Saturday afternoon and enjoying myself till Monday morning.

Only nine months had gone since Cousin Sophie's death, but to a girl of eleven those nine months were as many years. Occasional letters came to me from Trostnikovo, but they were like so many distant echoes. Nina wrote that Nastia and Uncle Basil were now formally engaged, that little Lisa called her favourite doll 'Katia' and refused to go to bed without her, and that Kolia had made up his mind to go into the Guards. Nina wrote about their lessons and their amusements, and always added that everybody missed me badly. In my replies I told her a lot about our house at Tver and Zvietkovo and not so much about Dubky. Mademoiselle Berg's letters were rather more informative than Nina's. A neighbour's daughter, one Natalie Rostovzeva, was now Nina's playmate, and Lili Lukanova, together with a distant cousin, were now frequent visitors at Trostnikovo. Old Lizbeth and Grand-maman had died during the summer. Volodia and Kolia were already in Kiev. But a great many unfamiliar names stole in and out of Mademoiselle Berg's letters. In brief, many things were happening at Trostnikovo in which I could never share, and that did not trouble me in the least. Far more than nine months in time and seven hundred miles in distance lay between that life and myself.

When Nina wrote rather naïvely: 'Is your stepmother very strict? I hear that she is beautiful,' I wanted to answer: 'But she is not a stepmother. She is truly my mamma and I love her,' but somehow I had no words to describe any of it. Nina was perfectly happy with her Natalie, Lili and Nadia. Once she had been happy with me. But that page was finished and turned over.

'I am going to school in the autumn,' I wrote to her, and did not quite like her reaction: 'What school? Natalie and Lili say there are no schools in Russia for girls like us—except in Moscow and St. Petersburg. Haven't you got a governess?' And I cannot now remember that I told her anything about Madame Guinter's place.

The house was well known to me by sight. It stood in the main square of Tver, an ochre-coloured, three-storied building, rather meanly windowed, with a big garden behind running right down to the river. Its chocolate-painted front door stood always closed. The ground floor windows were rather sumptuously curtained in deep red damask. Those on the first and second floors had dingy brown rep.

Madame Guinter was the widow of a petty customs official in the Baltic Provinces, and she had two maiden sisters living with her—Julia and Emilie. She must have been a very shrewd woman. A small *pensionnat* like hers would have been swamped in St. Petersburg or Moscow. She chose to strike her roots at Tver and she had no competitors there. The school prospered from the beginning in spite of Madame Guinter's innovations. It was certainly a school for daughters of nobility and gentry, but she did not refuse to take in pupils from among the merchant class. Such a policy might easily have led to failure. Surprisingly enough, it did not.

I should here explain that when I was a little girl, there was a gulf fixed between people like my own father and anyone engaged in trade. I knew about it and it always seemed funny to me. Trade meant buying and selling. Uncle Nicholas and all his neighbours certainly sold timber and cattle. So did Madame Khitrovó. So did my own father. Corn from Dubky and Zvietkovo, to say nothing of other things, often appeared at the Tver market, and I could not see any difference between that and a clothier's or a grocer's shop. But from the social sense, the difference stood for an insurmountable barrier. I believe that *kouptzy*, i.e. merchants, were often far more wealthy than any of us, but bags of gold as such did not matter.

I remember a timber merchant who once called at Zvietkovo to see my father. His horses were far more magnificent than any animals in our own stables, and one of our grooms told Andrew that Lapotkin dined off silver and had endowed quite a few monasteries in the neighbourhood. But Lapotkin entered the house through a back door and was seen by my father in a little room which served as estate office. There would not have been any hand-shaking, and Lapotkin would never have been invited to sit down. He himself would have thought it odd if he had been treated as

169

an equal.

Yet Madame Guinter was something of a genius in her generation. She certainly insisted on good manners and she and her sister Julia were exemplars of courtesy, but social origins meant very little to her. Two countesses and a princess were among her pupils but not even the maids ever addressed them by their titles.

And, unlike a great many heads of private schools at the time, Madame Guinter did not cheat the parents. The elegantly printed curriculum told no fairy stories. She employed a Frenchman to teach French and university men for other subjects. Mademoiselle Julia taught German, music and needlework. Monsieur Serbin's recommendation had certainly weighed with my father.

One golden October morning my little trunk and myself were deposited in the dim narrow hall of the house with the chocolate-painted front door. The maid who opened it looked so starchily grim that in sudden confusion I mistook our footman's hand for my stepmother's.

'It will be all right, *báryshna,*' muttered the man. He divested me of my coat, and made towards the door.

Outside stood our carriage, the two bays, Orlik and Krivoy, and Dimitry, the coachman, on the box, waiting to take my stepmother back to our house. Inside my trunk lay a big parcel of goodies so carefully prepared by our old cook, Michael, and boxed of sweets sent by Madame Khitrovó and Natalie. It helped me to remember them at that moment. Would they all have to be given up if I begged to be taken back home? So frightened was I of that sour-faced maid that I decided to risk it.

At home they had already dressed me in the Guinter uniform—a plain brown wool frock, black pinafore, and a brief white cape edged with lace. The maid wore unpleasing grey cotton, and there stood my elegant stepmother in a pale blue bonnet and a grey velvet cloak trimmed with ermine...

'Mamma,' I stammered in French, 'please let us drive back

home. I am scared. It is so dark here, and the woman does not look kind.'

'Now don't be foolish, Katia,' my stepmother replied. 'I know that before the day is over, you will have made at least one friend, and Madame Guinter is a very kindly woman.'

Our footman had vanished. The door was closed, and the grey cotton began moving towards the well of the hall. Another door was opened. I clutched my stepmother's hand and followed her through a very long room where a crowd of brown-frocked girls at once stopped their laughter and chatter and dropped quick little curtsies to my stepmother. Somewhere behind I heard a gasp, followed by a muttered:

'I say, girls, isn't she lovely?'

Never in all my life had I seen so many girls together. I was far too shy to turn round, but by the time we reached Madame Guinter's private drawing-room I forgot to feel troubled by the maid's sour face.

I can still see that room. Its ugliness made itself stay in the memory down the years. Deep red damask curtains, furniture covered with rather sickly yellow rep, bright blue walls, and masses of wax flowers under glass! The carpet was green, and all the tables were covered with some plushy purple stuff. Out of a deep armchair rose a portly elderly woman. She wore a gown of heliotrope silk and a pale brown shawl. The face under a tall lilac cap looked very kind, but I stepped back when I saw a fat pug at her feet sit up, and heard him snarl.

'Don't worry,' Madame Guinter smiled at me, 'his bark and his bite are far apart, as they say in England, so I believe.'

Not quite reassured, I kept close to my stepmother's chair whilst she discussed the business preliminaries with my future headmistress.

It was the briefest of all brief discussions, and Madame Guinter, having signed one or two documents, turned to me again.

'Now you belong here, my dear child, and we mean to keep you busy and happy. I believe your German is very good?'

'Yes, Madame,' I answered almost in a whisper.

'But you have never been to school before, have you? I have pupils who are good—and pupils who are naughty, and I hope you won't make friends with those.'

Embarrassed, I did not know what to say. My stepmother came to my rescue.

'She has had her two brothers for playmates, Madame Guinter, and neither of my sons is given to much naughtiness.'

But here she glanced at the clock. Madame Guinter leant forward and rang the bell.

'Frau von Almedingen's carriage, Matilda,' she said to the sour-faced maid. 'Now, *meine hochgnädigste Frau*, I feel sure that your daughter will distinguish herself at the Christmas examinations.'

My stepmother kissed me, shook hands with Madame Guinter, and vanished. Alone in the big, over-furnished room, I rather wanted to cry. I was also impatient and curious. What was going to happen next? I remembered my little trunk and its treasures. Where had they taken it?

'Now come and meet your future friends,' said Madame Guinter, her plump hand on my shoulder. 'A lesson is to start in twenty minutes. We work hard here.'

Before I knew where I was I found myself in the long room, girls on my right hand and girls on my left, and a barrage of questions welcomed me.

'What is your name? Have you come as a full boarder? Where do you live? Who was that beautiful lady with you?'

'My mother,' I replied boldly and proudly, and a red-haired, freckled girl about my own age burst out laughing.

'Your mother? How can she be? She looks much too young. How old are you?'

'I am going to be twelve at the end of the month.'

'She is much too young to be your mother.'

'And what about yours?' I parried, and the red-haired girl bit her lip.

'I don't remember mine. She died when I was quite tiny.'

And at once I was drawn to her. By the end of that first day Lydia and I were sworn friends, and she was the naughtiest girl at that school.

'You have met Azor, haven't you?'

'Azor?'

'Yes,' and the red-haired girl tumbled down on the floor, bent her head, and barked once or twice. 'The cleverest dog in the whole world!' she announced, rising and rumpling her hair. 'So Madame Guinter thinks. If I had my way, I would poison his dinner any day. He sleeps, snarls and smells... A beastly creature—but he is too fat to walk into the classroom. That is a blessing. Would you like to hear him again?'

And down she went for the second time, snarling and barking. We all laughed, when suddenly a younger edition of Madame Guinter appeared in the room.

Mademoiselle Julia did not laugh. Severely gowned in dark blue, her hair tightly plaited on the top of her head, she walked up to the red-haired girl.

'Must you be such a clown, Lydia, in front of a new pupil, too? What will Katia think of us all?'

Lydia instantly apologized. Privately, I thought it was great fun.

The bell rang. Some fifteen seniors made for one of the two classrooms. Some twenty odd juniors, including myself, made for another. I was shown my place. The master came in, a tall, portly priest in a purple cassock. It was to be Catechism and Church History.

I sat at the end of a bench in front. I felt terribly excited.

'This is my first day at school,' I thought, 'and it is wonderful! I mean to work very hard... I wonder if these girls

173

know as much history as I do? . . . What a lot there will be to tell Mademoiselle Berg in my next letter—I will describe Madame Guinter's drawing-room, and in German, too . . . I do like that Lydia. What fun she is! I must ask Mamma to invite her. I wonder if she is a day-pupil?' My musings were interrupted by Mademoiselle Julia's shocked voice:

'Katia! Katia von Almedingen! The master is speaking to you. Get up at once and answer him, child.'

Scarlet to the lobes of my ears, I jumped up. I had no idea what answer I was supposed to make. Luckily, Father Alexis proved to be a kindly man.

'Nobody can help thinking of their home on the very first day at school,' he smiled. 'Now, young lady, can you tell me anything about Joseph?'

I breathed freely. The story of Joseph and his brethren had been my favourite for years, and the priest did not have to prompt me once. His 'Thank you, excellent!' filled me with deep satisfaction, and I sat down, conscious of having climbed the first rung of a very long ladder.

There was no other lesson before dinner, and the first sight of the long vaulted refectory at the back of the house certainly damped my spirits. The room was dim, sparsely furnished with long tables and backless benches, and smelt of coffee and onions. Madame Guinter spared no efforts to have us well-taught by qualified masters, but in the matter of creaturely comforts she fell lamentably short of the standards I had been accustomed to. We slept hard, and stringent economies were the rule in the matter of ink, stationery and candles. Her youngest sister, Mademoiselle Emilie, was matron, housekeeper and cook in one. Our dinners and suppers were so many variations on the theme of milk, turnips, potatoes and onions. How I came to loathe those everlasting milk puddings, thinly spiced with cinnamon! Lydia made fun of the dull food, and I soon came to echo her.

However, there were week-ends at home, and I would get

back to Madame Guinter's with a comfortable hamper to sustain me during the lean days ahead.

I enjoyed the school hugely. Lydia and I became friends within the very first week. She was indeed the naughtiest girl at Madame Guinter's, but she was never at the bottom of the class. We were friends. We were also rivals in the best sense of the word.

The school was certainly good for me. My vanity was fed whenever I was praised for my successes in German and in history, but arithmetic, needlework and very elementary botany were my enemies. In particular, the beastly noughts always let me down—I could not even divide a thousand by ten! Arithmetic was our last lesson on Saturday afternoons. The master would depart at the sound of the bell but we were not allowed to leave until we had finished the problems set us. Oh, the agony of that last half-hour! The piece of crumbling chalk held in my hot fingers, the voices of my friends hurrying down the passage, the knowledge that the maid was waiting for me and that the carriage was outside the door, and there I would sit, tears misting my eyes, struggling with the beastly weights of equally detestable cheeses, apples and potatoes. At last, by a sheer miracle, the problem would be solved, the slate carried across the room for Mademoiselle Julia's inspection, and I would be free— till Monday morning.

That winter passed swiftly. About Easter, Madame Guinter had a stroke, and her sisters decided to close the school. Early in May my family and I migrated to Zvietkovo for the summer, Nicholas soon joining us there. What a heavenly summer it was! To begin with, the weather stayed perfect. Then my stepmother and I drew closer and closer together, and—best of all—my brothers and I spent whole days together in unbroken amity. Not once did Nicholas have to remind me that Andrew, being the youngest, needed our care. All three of us together went mushroom-hunting, fishing, walking, spent hours in the poultry-yard, with me

175

always keeping at a respectful distance from the turkey-cock. Nothing but thunder would send Andrew and me indoors. We simply clutched at each day as it came, and we refused to think about August.

Of course, there were tiresome dinner-parties at Dubky, and other occasions when, dressed in my best muslin, I had to join my parents in the carriage and drive to some neighbouring house, but that did not happen too often.

Strawberry-time and raspberry-time came and went, and the trees took to yellowing because we were in August; and those were our last weeks at home. Soon Nicholas would be returning to the Pages Corps in St. Petersburg, and Andrew and I would be leaving for Moscow, he to enter the Junior Cadet School and I—the Catherine Nobility Institute, one of the schools—the first founded by Catherine the Great in 1764—where pupils were not allowed to go home for holidays at all. They usually entered at nine, the course lasting seven years. I was nearly thirteen at the time. It was not at all easy to be accepted as a pupil at one of those places and, on first hearing about it, my stepmother and I had been very pleased.

'I am sure you will leave Catherine's with high honours, darling, and it will be less than four years for you. And Papa and I will come and see you at least four times a year.'

But now we were in August. Honours, gold medals had all lost their glamour. In the morning of our last day I wept like a four-year-old. The future loomed like a dark, unknown country. Andrew found me in my room and began howling in his turn. To make everything worse, Madame Khitrovó arrived and took to arguing with my father about Andrew.

'He is such a baby... The discipline there is just cruel, and think of that dreadful uniform—the collar will choke him! Why don't you wait for another two years and have him enter the Alexander Lyceum? Is it not enough for you to have one son in the army?'

My father said nothing at all in reply to her strictures. He looked out of the window and suggested that we might dine out of doors that day. Madame Khitrovó did not stay to dinner, and were we not glad to kiss her good-bye?

Somehow or other it was morning again. I am not sure if any of us ate much breakfast, but neither Andrew not I shed tears at table. I think we had begun looking forward to all the wonders of Moscow. Andrew had never been there and I could hardly remember it, but Nicholas had much to tell us of the Kremlin, the palaces, the churches, and a most marvellous bell—so big and heavy that it had never been hoisted on to a belfry. 'You will see—it is just standing there in the Red Square—"Tsar-Bell" they call it.'

The horses were waiting. The entire household and the village people were there to wish us God-speed. My throat very tight, I clasped my stepmother's hand as we came out of the front door. I saw poor Andrew's little podgy fist rubbing his eyes. I heard Nicholas's urgent whisper: 'Head up, little man! Wave and smile at them all! It is such fun—travelling post!' And Andrew smiled a very watery smile and waved his fat hand as hard as he could.

So did I, and then we were in the carriage, the bays trotting towards the gateway and the high road. At the first corner, tall elms screened the dear roof of Zvietkovo—not to be seen again for nearly four years.

# Epilogue

The story of a little girl is told. Much of my childhood slipped away on that day in August 1842 when I entered the gloomy vaulted hall of the Catherine Nobility Institute in Moscow. The first day was a nightmare, since—according to tradition—a 'new girl' was teased and tormented unmercifully. The girls taunted me about my surname, my way of walking, the colour of my hair and eyes. I had been imprudent enough to pack a doll among the few belongings the pupils were allowed to keep in their lockers. For several days they called me 'ninny' and told the servants waiting at table to have all my food cut into small pieces since I had not yet cut my first tooth!

But the misery did not last. In the end, I was very happy there.

I have told the story of my early years as I remember it. It may seem remote in time, yet it is still close to me.

Cousin Sophie had a very old friend who sometimes stayed at Trostnikovo. She came during Cousin Sophie's last illness. Once, from the open doorway, I heard her calm voice: 'Don't fret about the child, Sophie. God will take care of her.' Now, in the evening of my life, I know those words have come true.

# GLOSSARY

BÁRYSHNA            'Miss'—diminutive. From *Baryna*—
                    'Madame'.

BORTCH              Beetroot soup served with cream.

KÓKOSHNIK           Women's traditional headgear, dating from
                    the Middle Ages.

SÁMOVAR             Tea-urn.

TRÓYKA              Three horses harnessed together.

NITCHÉVO SEBE       'So-so! Might be worse!'

SÁRAFAN             Women's traditional dress, dating from the
                    Middle Ages.

RÚSSKAYA            A Russian national dance.

BRÍTCHKA            A roomy hooded carriage drawn by three
                    horses, sometimes by four.